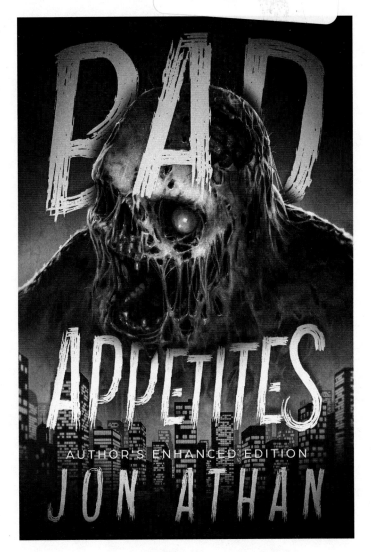

BAD APPETITES

AUTHOR'S ENHANCED EDITION

JON ATHAN

For more information on this book or the author, please visit www.jon-athan.com. General inquiries are welcome.

Facebook: https://www.facebook.com/AuthorJonAthan
Twitter: @Jonny_Athan
Instagram: @AuthorJonnyAthan
Email: info@jon-athan.com

Cover illustration by Pedro Bianchi Guerra: https://www.artstation.com/predo
Front cover typography and logo by: https://miblart.com/
Proofreading provided by Karen Bennett: kbennett4653@gmail.com

ISBN: 9798404923650
Second Edition

ALSO BY JON ATHAN

WARNING

This book contains scenes of intense violence and some disturbing themes. Some parts of this book may be considered violent, cruel, disturbing, or unusual. Certain implications may also trigger strong emotional responses. This book is also *not* intended for those easily offended or appalled. Please enjoy at your own discretion.

CONTENTS

1

THE LITTLE VOICE

You can't do this, you slob, the little voice in Cindy Moore's head said. *What were you thinking? You don't belong here. You never did and you never will. Give up. Give up. Give up.*

Cindy breathed like she was in labor, taking in huge gulps of air. She was walking on a treadmill, but she wasn't dying from exhaustion or even out of breath. She was just trying to muster the courage to run. She had already finished her stretches and her warm-up exercise, but she couldn't start jogging. Her insecurities held her back.

She frowned as she stared at her reflection in the mirror in front of the treadmill. Her blonde hair was tied in a messy bun, strands sticking out in every direction. Her blue eyes were so dim that they looked gray. Although she liked her outfit, the sportswear was comfortable and stylish, the clothing couldn't hide what she hated about herself.

The fat.

It was everywhere. Most of the extra weight accumulated on her belly, but it hung from her flabby arms and chin, too. She was 23 years old, and her weight fluctuated around 280 pounds. Whenever she looked at her reflection, she only saw a giant blob of flesh staring back at her. And she felt like everyone else saw that monstrous blob as well.

"This is so stupid," Cindy said, her voice barely perceptible over the gym's loud music. "Just run already, Cindy. You're wasting time."

She started swinging her arms back and forth. She looked like she was moving faster, but she was still walking. She glanced around at the other people in the gym. She was surrounded by people at many different points in their fitness journeys—young and old, brawny and weak, skinny and obese, and everything in between—but she only saw muscular men and beautiful, petite women around her.

She felt like the only overweight person in the building. A pang of envy put a sneer of bitterness on her face.

She thought: *We're all here to exercise. There's nothing wrong with running. I paid my fee. I got out of bed to do this. They can't stop me. I can only stop myself.*

"Screw it," she muttered. "Screw it all."

She tapped the PLUS sign on the treadmill. She

increased the speed to four miles per hour, accelerating to a brisk walk. She took a deep breath, then pressed the PLUS sign until she reached four-and-a-half miles per hour. She now looked like she was walking and jogging at the same time, her legs moving faster than her upper body.

If she increased the speed again, she would have had to start running or she would have been hurled off the treadmill. She took a swig of water from her bottle, then she pressed the PLUS sign again, closed her eyes, and jogged. For a brief moment, she felt good—free, optimistic, *euphoric*. Her world was more attractive when her eyes were closed.

But then curiosity started tugging on her eyelids. She heard the treadmill *clunking* and felt it shaking violently with each heavy step. The noise got so loud that she couldn't hear the generic gym music. It sounded like the treadmill was about to collapse. Her eyelids twitched open to slits. Tears blurred her vision and, as she closed her eyes again, a drop rolled down each rosy cheek.

She swiped at her face and sighed, then she opened her eyes wide. She gasped and nearly lost her footing, barely catching herself on the treadmill's handrails. She saw the human blob in the mirror again. This time, it looked like a fleshy rhinoceros-shaped human. She was frightened and revolted by her reflection. More tears flowed down her cheeks.

You're a monster, the little voice in her head said.

Won't be long until one of the employees drags you off that thing. You're going to break it, fat ass, and you can't afford it. Just stop. Stop it already.

Cindy wiped her cheeks and whispered, "I can't do this."

She looked to her right. A young man ran on a treadmill at six-and-a-half miles per hour just a few feet away. Big drops of sweat fell from his face and landed on the treadmill's display and control panel. Music blaring from his earbuds and his gaze fixed on his reflection, he was focused on his exercise. The rest of the world didn't matter to him.

Cindy slowed her treadmill to two miles per hour. She grabbed onto the handrail, bent over, and panted while walking. It took her more time to catch her breath than she spent running. She glanced around at the other guests. No one paid any attention to her. They were either concentrating on their exercises or focused on their cell phones.

Yet, she felt like she was being watched and judged by everyone. She heard their nasty comments in her head.

'*She's so fat and disgusting.*'

'*She's going to break that thing.*'

'*She smells so bad.*'

'*What is she even doing here?*'

'*That pig must have gotten lost looking for a buffet.*'

The voices in her head came from men and women, but she had never heard any of the other customers speak. Some of the other guests were panting, but no one was talking. Aside from the noise from the equipment and the music, the gym was quiet. Yet, her insecurities planted seeds of paranoia in her mind. She didn't trust anyone. She tightened her grip on the handrail and glared at the other guests.

If they're not saying it, they're thinking it, she thought.

"A–Assholes," she muttered, her voice quivering. "A–All of you a–are assholes."

Upon noticing her erratic behavior, the young man next to her took out one of his earbuds and asked, "You okay?"

"Huh?"

"Are you okay?" the guy asked as he slowed his treadmill down to a walking pace.

"Oh. I–I'm fine."

"You sure?"

Cindy opened her mouth to speak, but the words wouldn't come out. So, she smiled awkwardly at him. The man returned the smile and nodded at her. He took a swig of his water, put his earbud in, then continued his run. Cindy cast her eyes down at her treadmill's display. She was baffled by the man's gentleness.

If she learned anything through her years of being bullied at school, it was one thing: *If it's too good to be true, it most likely isn't good or true to begin with.*

She watched the runner from the corner of her eyes. She wondered if he was trying to mock her or if he was interested in her romantically. There was no in-between in her warped mind.

She said, "Just act natural."

Cindy turned off the treadmill and wiped the sweat off her face with a small towel. Then she turned to face the young guy and waved at him. He didn't notice her. Cindy dropped her arm so fast that she slapped her thigh hard. The rejection, although unintentional, was humiliating, like waving at a person who was waving at someone else.

"Why did I do that?" she whimpered.

She jogged across the gym, running past the other treadmills, the seated chest and shoulder press equipment, and the stationary bikes. Sunshine poured into the gym through the glass doors at the exit and the surrounding window walls. Just as she approached the finish line, her feet tangled and she spilled to the floor between the front desk and the exit.

Staring down at the tan rubber tiles, Cindy muttered, "Shit, shit, shit." Eyes glazed with tears, she glanced over her shoulder and hissed, "Leave me alone."

To her utter surprise, there was no one there. She was expecting to find a crowd of people surrounding her, pointing and laughing at her like high school bullies. It was a rare moment where she was relieved to be ignored. At the same time, she felt alone—abandoned and rejected. Even the employee at the front desk, who was answering a customer's questions on the phone, missed Cindy's fall.

No one offered her a helping hand.

She grabbed her towel and water bottle, then struggled to her feet. She walked out of the gym and went to the black sedan parked near the entrance. A cool breeze caressed her sweaty body. She sat in the driver's seat and pressed her moist forehead against the steering wheel. She waited in silence for a minute.

She said, "They wanted to laugh, but they couldn't. They didn't want to be 'rude' or 'mean' in front of me because it wouldn't look good for them. They're probably laughing now, though. Yeah, they are. I know it. They're rotten on the inside. Those... Those bitches. Those stupid bitches. They were just waiting until I left so they could talk about me. It's always like that. Always the same crap. Always..."

She tended to talk to herself when she was alone. It was hard for her to keep her negative thoughts locked away in her head.

She let out a shaky breath. Her face spasmed, then crumpled. She lowered her head and sobbed, unable to contain her emotions. She didn't want the world to see her cry—*again*. Society had laughed at her enough for one lifetime.

Between her raspy breaths, she said, "I... hate them. I hate... everything and everyone. Why can't I just... just disappear? Just take me away from... from all of this bullshit. I'm begging you. Take me away before I do something I'll regret."

She sat there and sniveled for a few minutes. She used her gym towel to wipe her face before leaning back in her seat. Upon catching a glimpse of her reflection, she moved the rearview mirror. She didn't want to see herself. Her cries were sincere. She wanted to disappear, but she knew the way the world worked. Society needed her as a steppingstone for other people.

Cindy frowned at the steering wheel as she thought about life. No matter how badly she wanted, she couldn't leave. She had a job to do, she had bills to pay, she had dreams to pursue. She thought about her boyfriend, Joseph Madrigal, too. She was on the cusp of giving up, but she wasn't quite ready to disappear.

She turned her attention to the gym's entrance. A petite redheaded woman in a black sports bra and matching leggings stood outside of the gym. She held her cell phone out in front of her with her arm slightly elevated. Cycling through different facial expressions, she took dozens of selfies to share one later with the world. She stood on the street to ensure the gym was visible in the background.

"Look at me, everyone, I went to the gym to take a picture of myself," Cindy said mockingly while reversing out of her parking space.

Hit her, the little voice in Cindy's head said as she put her car in drive.

She hesitated, her foot resting on the gas pedal. The other woman stood in her crosshairs, completely unaware of the terrible thoughts festering in Cindy's mind. There was nothing stopping Cindy from ramming her with her car and then driving off. Then she saw the young guy from the treadmill exit the gym, tearing her from her hate-fueled trance. She turned right and drove off.

Watching the redhead from the rearview mirror, she said, "Good luck with your Instagram 'modeling,' bitch."

2

THE MOVIE DATE

CINDY STOOD NEXT TO A FOUNTAIN AT THE CENTER OF the plaza with her arms crossed over her chest, water splashing behind her. The sun fell beyond the tall movie theater in front of her, the yellow-orange light beating down on her upper body. To her right, people sipped coffee and sugary beverages at a Starbucks. And to her left, families ate ice cream at a Cold Stone Creamery. Customers walked in and out of the theater —alone, in groups of friends, with their families, *with their partners*.

You don't belong here, either, the little voice in Cindy's head said. Her inner voice always said that whenever she wasn't home. The voice continued. *You can't be happy like them if you're not happy with yourself or him*.

Her gaze wandered to the movie ticket kiosks near the entrance of the theater. Her boyfriend, Joseph, stood there, tapping away at a touchscreen to purchase their tickets. He was a short, overweight man, about a hundred pounds heavier than Cindy. His hair was buzz cut and his fuzzy beard mostly covered his neck. Like his girlfriend, he was dressed in baggy clothing. He exuded a friendly, confident aura, though. There wasn't a hateful bone in his body.

"But I love him," Cindy whispered, replying aloud to her inner voice.

He's worse than you, the little voice said. *You're better off without him.*

"Got the tickets," Joseph said as he approached her. "C'mon, I need to buy some snacks before the movie. Don't want to miss the previews."

"Yeah, um... Yeah, let's go."

An employee checked their tickets at the door before allowing them into the lobby. Cindy examined the movie posters on the walls and the large cardboard standees in the corners of the room. She wasn't interested in the latest superhero extravaganzas, haunted house movies, or romantic comedies. Her upper lip began to curl back in a sneer of jealousy. She envied the beautiful actors in every movie.

She didn't see anyone who looked like herself in any of the posters—no human blobs in sight. And whenever she noticed any overweight actors in any movies, they were used as comic relief in slapstick gags or portrayed unfavorably.

Even the 'ugly' ones are gorgeous, she thought. *It's not fair.*

"What do you want, babe?" Joseph asked.

His voice snapped her out of her hypnotic state. She looked at the snack bar. She wanted to say something like: '*Nothing, I'm on a diet.*' But then she caught a whiff of the buttery popcorn, fresh hot dogs, and tangy nacho cheese. Her taste buds tingled with excitement and goosebumps rashed out on her arms. Her eyes went to the boxes of candy and chocolate on the shelves under the cash register.

She swallowed the lump in her throat, then said, "I... I think I'm going to stick to my diet this time. Go ahead and get whatever you want. I'll wait for you."

"You sure? A little popcorn never hurt anyone. I'll even order it without butter if you want."

"I'm fine."

"*Really?*"

Cindy laughed nervously, then said, "I think I can survive without food for an hour or two."

Joseph shrugged and said, "Okay, have it your way."

He walked up to the cashier. Hawk-eyed, Cindy watched as her boyfriend ordered his snacks. He bought a medium-sized popcorn with butter, a box of Milk Duds to mix with his popcorn, two hot dogs, and a large *diet* soda for himself. It all added up to approximately 1,650 calories. She admired his ability to ignore other people's opinions on his weight and diet.

She put a fake smile on her face, wrapped her arm around him, and grabbed his soda in her free hand to help him out. They went to their auditorium. A few couples and families already sat in their seats. Only one person—a young guy—sat alone.

Joseph beckoned to Cindy and said, "C'mon, we're in the middle of Row J."

"Middle?" Cindy repeated. She sighed, then muttered, "Why do you always get middle seats?"

"They're the best seats in the house. It's scientifically proven."

Cindy liked the view from the center, but she hated sitting there because of the other guests. She didn't like drawing attention to herself. A frown pulled her lips down as she spotted a young couple—the lovey-dovey type—in Row J. While squeezing past them to get to their seats, she heard them grunting and groaning and scoffing.

"Sorry," Cindy squeaked out.

The couple didn't say a word to her. It was a minor inconvenience after all. They went back to their own conversation as soon as Cindy and Joseph were out of their way.

Cindy sat to Joseph's left, away from the other couple. She didn't want to see them during the movie. She was anxious and bitter already. Negative thoughts swirled around in her head. She felt them in there, like a field of tumors blossoming across her brain. And each growth was like a small megaphone, amplifying the voice in her head.

It wasn't so little anymore.

You don't belong here! her inner voice screamed.

She closed her eyes and breathed deeply while rubbing her temple. Her trembling fingers slid across her sweaty brow.

The sound of rustling aluminum foil interrupted her concentration.

She glanced to her right. Her teeth went straight to her lower lip. Joseph had unwrapped a hot dog. It was decorated with parallel stripes of ketchup and mustard. He licked his lips and took a whiff of it, practically salivating like a hungry dog. Cindy heard the growling from her small intestine. She hadn't eaten anything since her bowl of oatmeal in the morning.

In a strangled voice, she said, "Hey, Joseph, um... I know I'm going to sound annoying, but... but..."

Her voice faltered as she hesitated. Her nostrils flared as the scent of the hot dog rose to her face. She gulped.

Joseph smirked and asked, "What? What is it?"

Cindy gave a twitchy smile and said, "I know it sounds *so* annoying. Like, *totally* annoying or maybe even crazy. And I'm sorry about that, but... can I have a bite? A little one? Please?"

"Cindy, Cindy, Cindy. You didn't think all of this food was for me, did you?"

'*Yes.*' Cindy sucked her lips into her mouth to stop herself from blurting out that word.

Joseph chuckled, then said, "All right, I would have eaten it all if I was wrong, but I knew you'd want a taste. That's why I ordered two hot dogs. One for me, one for you. Here. Go ahead, take it."

Cindy blushed and laughed. Her boyfriend knew her very well. She felt his tremendous love for her. She appreciated his nonjudgmental and caring attitude, but she was worried he might have been enabling her poor eating habits. Yet, she couldn't resist the food. She kissed his cheek, then accepted the hot dog.

She leaned back in her seat and unwrapped the rest of the aluminum foil, as if she were tearing the wrapping paper off a Christmas gift. She took a big bite, chewed the mouthful for a few seconds, then took another bite. And just like that, she was halfway done. Her eyes stung and tears clung to her eyelids.

Joseph squinted at her. Although the auditorium was dimly lit, he could see the tears shimmering in his girlfriend's eyes and hear her sniffles.

He leaned in closer to her and whispered, "What's wrong, Cin? You okay?"

Cindy gulped the food down, then said, "I'm fine. Everything's fine. I'm just so happy to be here right now. My day sucked and it... it feels like a dream to be here."

She wiped at the wetness on her cheeks with her sleeves, then gazed into Joseph's eyes. She couldn't hold eye contact for long, though. She was about to lie to him, and she couldn't do it while looking at him. She eyed her hot dog.

She put a phony smile on her face and said, "A dream date with my dream man. It's perfect."

"That's nothing to cry over, babe. But it's romantic. I think you're going to make me tear up, too. Maybe after... Oh, wait, the movie's starting. Shh, shh."

Cindy looked up at the movie trailers playing on the projection screen. Accompanied by blaring horns and remixed pop music, the trailers spoiled each movie, giving everything away in less than three minutes. It didn't bother her very much, though. Depression had invaded her mind, poisoning her thoughts and muddling her memories. She couldn't even remember what movie they were about to watch.

In the periphery of her vision, she saw someone standing next to the emergency exit down the stairs to her right. She felt like the person was staring at her.

No, no, no, she told herself. *It's just someone looking for their seat.*

But she couldn't shake the feeling of being watched. It made her stomach rise and the hairs at the nape of her neck stand erect.

Without turning her head, her eyes crawled across the projection screen until her vision settled on the person. Her pupils dilated with fear and a short, shaky breath escaped her lips. A woman stood near the emergency exit. In the dark auditorium, she was partially illuminated by the flashing from the movie trailers and the green glow from the emergency sign above the door.

The first thing Cindy noticed was the woman's lack of clothes. She was nude, revealing her gaunt figure— more bone than flesh. Like a corpse, she was alarmingly pale. Frizzy, thinning hair enveloped her head. She was pointing at Cindy, her limbs shaking uncontrollably. She looked like she was about to fall apart.

Cindy glanced over her shoulder. No one sat behind her. She looked back at the emergency exit and furrowed her brow. The woman was gone. She checked the stairs to her left and right, then observed the seats in front of her. She couldn't find the mysterious woman anywhere in the auditorium. She squeezed her eyes shut and rubbed them.

Joseph asked, "What's wrong?"

"I–I'm okay."

"You don't look so good."

Cindy said, "It's just a... a little headache." She opened her eyes, smiled at him, and whispered, "I'm better now."

"Are you–"

"The trailers are finally over. Let's watch."

Trying to act natural, she took another bite of her hot dog and turned her attention to the projection screen. Joseph shrugged off her unusual behavior, munching on his popcorn and watching the movie. Throughout the entire movie, Cindy kept glancing at the emergency exit. The same thought ran through her head: *Who was that woman?*

Cindy stared vacantly at the projection screen as the closing credits rolled with a somber score in the background. The other guests started to depart as soon as the credits started rolling. Some of them complained about the movie's pace and others discussed its twist ending. The lovey-dovey couple in Row J stayed behind to snap some selfies.

Cindy paid them no mind, although she observed each and every audience member. She was on the lookout for the nude woman.

"You ready to head out?" Joseph asked as he rubbed her thigh.

"Not yet. You know I like to wait until it gets empty. It's too stuffy moving around with all of these people in here. Let's just wait a minute."

"Sure, whatever you say."

There was an awkward moment of silence between them as Cindy continued scanning the auditorium.

Joseph asked, "So, what did you think of the movie? You like it?"

"Yeah. It was sad. I like sad movies."

"Really? Why?"

Cindy wanted to say: '*Because I'm sad.*' She didn't want to alarm her boyfriend, though.

She said, "Because they make me feel something."

"I guess I get what you mean. 'Happy' movies can make you feel something, too, y'know? I thought the movie was fantastic. Much better than the usual crap that's been coming. It had that..."

Joseph's words became nothing but a garble of noise in Cindy's ears. She watched his lips flap and his soft face jiggle like jelly, but she didn't listen to a word out of his mouth. She liked the movie, but she was more concerned about her physical and mental health. She couldn't stop hating herself and she couldn't stop thinking about the nude woman. She felt like she was eating herself to death while bullying herself into a never-ending state of depression. She was her own worst enemy.

"I'm falling apart," she said, barely audible.

"Huh?"

Cindy shook her head and stuttered, "No–Nothing. Just, um... We can go now. Yeah, let's go."

"Sure."

They held hands and walked out of the auditorium, throwing their trash away in the garbage bin in the corridor. In the lobby, through the tall wall windows, they noticed the dark sky and bright plaza lights outside.

Cindy's eyes grew as she spotted another couple walking towards them. A smile—a *real* smile—stretched across her face.

"Charlotte!" she called out enthusiastically.

Charlotte Torres was Cindy's closest friend. They had been friends since middle school—ten years and counting. Although she was usually bitter towards everyone, Cindy cherished her relationship with Charlotte. She appreciated her advice and kindness and honesty. Charlotte wasn't the type of person to put on airs or disrespect others. She was a true friend with a heart of gold.

She was a beautiful, curvy woman with curly black hair and light brown eyes. She was confident, but she had her fair share of insecurities—everyone did. Cindy liked her modesty. It made her feel better about her own insecurities. It made her comfortable around Charlotte. She didn't have to feel like she was competing with her or being judged around her.

"Cindy!" Charlotte exclaimed as she approached them. "Hey, hon, how've you been?"

They hugged.

Cindy said, "I'm good. Just working and..."

She didn't know what else to say. She didn't have a lot going on in her life. Then she noticed Charlotte's fiancé, Michael Barnes, next to them. He shook Joseph's hand and said something to him, but Cindy didn't catch it. She was too busy gawking at him. He was her 'type,' her dream man—tall, strong, and stylish.

Her face flushed, she said, "Oh and, you know, working on losing a couple of pounds before your big day."

"*What?*" Charlotte said in disbelief. "Seriously, Cin? You don't have to worry about that. You look fine, hun.

You're going to steal the show. Might even make some of the guys go crazy."

"Whoa, whoa, whoa," Joseph said. "I'm standing right here, ladies. Cin doesn't need the 'guys' to go crazy for her. If they go crazy, then *I'm* going to go crazy. I don't think you want to see that."

"No one wants to see that, Joe," Michael said.

Charlotte asked, "So, what did you guys watch?"

Joseph started yapping about the movie before Cindy could even remember the film's title. She didn't pay attention to their conversation. She crossed her arms and looked around the busy lobby, growing fidgety as other customers walked around them. They were all laughing and chatting. She felt like they were all watching her—talking about her, *mocking her*. She heard people saying her name from every direction. Then she shuddered as she looked at the posters and standees. She felt like the characters in the inanimate objects were staring at her, too.

Every eye in the lobby was glued to her body.

"No spoilers, please!"

Charlotte's voice brought Cindy back to reality. She laughed along with the others, despite missing the entire conversation.

Charlotte said, "We're going to have to start doing double dates so Joseph doesn't spoil everything for us. What do you think, Cindy? We can go out for dinner, catch a movie, go for a walk or hit a bar."

"Sounds nice," Joseph said. "*But*, I don't spoil *every-*

thing. Really, the movie trailers spoil more than I do these days."

"You just posted a spoiler yesterday on your Instagram Stories."

"Oh, c'mon, that movie came out last month."

Laughing, Charlotte said, "It came out last week."

"Really? Shit. Time's a funny thing, huh?"

Cindy coughed to interrupt them, then said, "That sounds great. We should totally set something up later. But I think I should start heading home now. I'm feeling a little tired. It's been a long week."

"Oh yeah, sounds good," Charlotte said. "I'll call you tomorrow. We can go out for lunch and a drink or two."

"Yeah, call me."

"Have a good night, guys."

Michael said, "Talk to you guys later."

Cindy smiled and waved at them as they split ways. The smile left her face as soon as she turned away from Charlotte. Joseph said his goodbyes, then followed Cindy out of the theater. He was her ride home.

3

HOME SWEET HOME

THE RED PICKUP TRUCK CRAWLED TO A STOP IN FRONT OF a four-story apartment building. Thin rays of light seeped past the blinds and curtains over some of the windows. Most of the apartments were dark, though. Across the street, in another apartment complex's parking lot, a group of teenagers sat in a sedan, smoking and listening to music.

It was a regular night.

From the driver's seat of the pickup truck, Joseph said, "We should, uh... probably talk, huh?"

Cindy stared blankly at the four-story apartment building. Its rustic brick exterior was dappled with bird shit and decorated with graffiti. In the alley next to the building, a decrepit tireless car was left on cinderblocks. It had been there for over a year. There was another clunker on cinderblocks in the parking lot across the street, too.

Her impoverished environment didn't do her poor mind any favors. Financial problems were known to exacerbate depressive and anxiety disorders.

"About what?" she replied.

"I think you know."

"The movie?"

"No, Cin, not the freakin' movie. We should talk about you and your feelings. You've been acting... different lately. I've been trying to help by giving you your space and letting you do you, but you're just not yourself. You've changed. I don't even recognize you sometimes, y'know? I guess I thought you might want to talk about it."

"Talking probably won't help."

"But it might."

"Even if I had something to say—and I'm not saying I do—you probably wouldn't understand anyway. Life is... complicated."

Joseph gave her a half-smile and said, "You never know, right?"

Fed up with his prying, Cindy clenched her fists and jaw. She held her breath to stop herself from screaming. She turned in her seat and glared at him. Despite her obvious frustration, he stayed calm and focused. He sincerely cared about her wellbeing. She unfurled her fists and let out a long exhale through her nose.

"*Fine,*" Cindy said, exasperated. "Let's talk about it —about *me*. Let's talk about my 'weight issues' and 'eating habits.' That's the polite way to say it, right? Let's talk about me weighing over *280* pounds. Let's talk about me being twice the size of most women. Maybe even *three* times the size of some of the women at my gym. Let's talk about... about..." Choking on a lump of anxiety, her voice wavered. She swallowed loudly, then said, "Let's talk about being bullied. Being bullied for years. Directly and indirectly. By others and by myself. Let's talk about having to take shit from *everyone* and never being able to throw shit back. Is that what you want to talk about?"

Joseph sat in stunned silence. He was expecting her to lash out at him, but he was still taken aback by her speech.

"Yeah," he said. "That's what I wanted to talk about. All that 'shit' you've been holding inside of you, you can throw it at me. I can take it, hon. Go ahead. Get it all off your chest."

"I know you can take it, Joe. I mean, shit, you're bigger than I am. You've been going through the same crap all your life. And I don't know how you do it. I guess you have thicker skin than me. Or maybe... maybe your *fat* just absorbs all of it. Maybe you just don't hear it through your *fat* ears. Maybe you're..."

She stopped mid-sentence, her mouth hanging agape. Her mind had finally caught up to her quick mouth. The voice coming out of her mouth reminded her of the little voice in her head.

She said, "I'm sorry. I–I don't know what I'm saying. I'm so sorry."

Unperturbed, Joseph shrugged and said, "It's fine. I'm good. I told you already, I can handle it."

"No, I was wrong. Dead wrong. I was just... I was putting everything on you. The types of things people say to me, that I say to myself, I was throwing it at you. I have self-esteem issues—*obviously*. I want to be thin or at least curvy like everyone else. I want to fit in, but I can't do that when my fat makes me stand out."

There was a short period of silence.

Cindy said, "Seriously, Joseph, you're not the problem. You're not even part of it. You're, like, the only good thing in my life. You and Charlotte. I'm just getting tired of all the bullshit out there. I'm tired of people staring and pointing and laughing and bullying. I'm starting to hate everyone and everything. I wish I could..."

Kill them, the little voice in her head said, finishing her sentence when she couldn't.

"Hate?" Joseph repeated. "That's a little strong, ain't it? I mean, I get it, but I don't want to see you fall. You know what I mean? I know there are a lot of assholes out there and I don't want to see you turn into one of 'em."

Stop it, Cindy thought in response to the little voice.

Blinking erratically, as if sending a message in morse code, she said, "I didn't mean it like that. I was just caught in my emotions. Forget about it."

Joseph studied her distraught demeanor. Her words didn't hurt him, but he felt her pain in his heart. He saw the hatred and depression festering within her. Depression was difficult to treat. He wasn't trained to help her, either. He worked as a Geek Squad agent at a Best Buy. He could fix her computer, but he couldn't heal her mind.

He said, "We can get you some help, Cin. We can talk to, um... to doctors about this. Professionals, y'know? I can pay for it, too. Really, you don't have to worry about money or anything like that."

Nose clogged with mucus, Cindy began to snuffle and tears crawled down her pink cheeks. She had thought about visiting psychiatrists and psychologists, but it all frightened her—the talking, the medication, the stigma.

She said, "I don't need a 'professional' to tell me what's wrong. I know how to fix my problems. I just need to focus on my exercise and diet. Everything else is a... a non-issue. It's just me over-thinking things."

"Are you sure?"

"I'm positive. I'm just emotional. It's normal, isn't it?"

"I guess so."

There was another brief moment of silence.

"Can I ask you something else?" Joseph said.

Cindy said, "I don't really want to talk about myself anymore."

"It's not really about you."

Cindy wiped her eyes with her sleeve and asked, "What is it then?"

"Do you hate me because of my weight?"

'*Yes.*' The little voice in Cindy's head almost escaped through her mouth again. She pulled her lips into her mouth and shook her head. She wasn't attracted to his figure, she disliked his obesity as much as she disliked her own, but she didn't outright *hate* him. It was more like a love-hate relationship, and she blamed herself for it.

She said, "Of course not. Jeez, of course not, Joseph. You're the only person I ever loved. I feel like a monster around everyone else, but you make me feel like a human. You make me feel loved and appreciated. I could never—*never*—hate you because of your weight, especially when I look the way I do. That would be so stupid, babe."

Joseph gazed into Cindy's eyes, but she didn't look back into his. He could tell she was lying. It was a white lie, a lie to protect him, but a *lie* nonetheless.

Cindy leaned closer to him, put her hands on his cheeks, and said, "I love you, sweetie. I love you with all of my heart. Thank you for listening to me. Thank you for taking care of me. And thank you for the perfect date." She kissed him, then she smirked and said, "We need to do this again. I'll call you tomorrow, okay?"

As Cindy climbed out of the truck, Joseph said, "All right. Call me if you need anything. I love you, Cin."

Walking to the entrance of the apartment building, Cindy waved back at him and said, "Love you, too. Good night."

"Good night."

She stopped on the porch and watched as Joseph drove away, making sure he was safe. Her heart was bruised, beaten black and blue by years of abuse, but she still had a little bit of compassion in her body.

***

The hinges squealed as the door slowly swung open. The dim light from the hallway poured into the dark studio apartment.

Cindy crossed the threshold and flicked a switch near the door. To her right, the light in the kitchen turned on, nearly illuminating the entire apartment. She closed and locked the door behind her, then tossed her bag on the kitchen counter. She went to the sink, filled a glass with tap water, then chugged it down. She refilled the cup and drank some more, then refilled it again—*and again.*

'You're not depressed. You just need to sleep eight hours a night and drink more water.' She had read that advice on Twitter. It came from a self-proclaimed millionaire health guru. Although she had been following his advice, guzzling down water every night as if trying to kill herself through water intoxication, nothing changed.

She was still depressed and still anxious.

After her fifth cup, she looked over the kitchen bar and inspected the apartment, as if she were afraid she had accidentally entered a stranger's home. There was a queen-sized bed in the middle of the room. Next to her nightstand, there was a tattered sofa. It was meant to seat two people, but Cindy and Joseph never fit on it together. Across from the sofa, there was a wide dresser with a 32-inch flat-screen television on top.

Her gaze traveled back to the foyer. Next to the entrance, a door led to the bathroom. She lived alone in the cramped apartment, but she still appreciated the privacy of her bathroom. It was her safe space.

She opened the refrigerator and looked inside. She found nothing but processed foods, sugary drinks, and leftovers from fast food restaurants.

With a wry smile, she whispered, "What's the point of saying I'm on a diet when I'm really not? I try to eat a salad, but then I just soak it in dressing. I drink so much water just to drink soda right after. I never..." Her voice cracked like a teenager's. She said, "I never change. Nothing ever changes, so why am I torturing myself like this? It's so stupid. I'm such an idiot. I'm a..."

A fat fucking idiot, the little voice in her head finished her sentence again.

She opened the freezer and pulled a tub of vanilla ice cream out. She put it on a counter, then took a jar of creamy peanut butter out of a cupboard. With a large spoon, she blended three big dollops of peanut butter into the ice cream. She carried the tub into her living room and flumped into her sofa. A cotton blanket over her legs, she put the tub on her lap and shoveled into the ice cream with her trusty spoon.

She only wanted to escape from her depression with her favorite dessert and some trashy TV. To her dismay, she found herself flipping through channel after channel of beautiful people. She didn't care about the celebrities' personal lives. Their struggles were irrelevant to her. All that mattered was that they were beautiful and they *appeared* happy—and that infuriated her.

She knew most actors were beautified through flawless makeup, professional lighting, and favorable camera angles, but she never really accepted it. She convinced herself that they were naturally perfect.

Face screwed up in a grimace and a mouth full of melting ice cream, she whined, "They're so beautiful. They get more and more and *more* beautiful every day. It's not fair. It's not fucking fair!"

She hurled the spoon at her TV. The image flickered and ice cream splashed across the display. She jumped to her feet, allowing the tub of ice cream to fall to the floor. Some goops of ice cream splattered on the shaggy carpet. She hurried to the bathroom and turned on the light. Her bulging eyes spun in their sockets as she examined the room.

"It's not fair," she murmured as she fell to her knees in front of her toilet. "It's never fair."

She pulled a glass digital weight scale from behind the toilet. She put it on the toilet seat, then grabbed the edge of the counter next to her and a towel hanging from a rack to pull herself up. She was short of breath from the slight exertion. She grabbed the scale and wobbled over to the sink.

She said, "You... You're the reason I hate myself every morning. I exercise, I try to diet, but you never drop. The number just keeps rising and rising! It's bullshit!"

Cindy screamed and flung the scale at the medicine cabinet's mirror. The mirror exploded, dozens of shards raining down into the sink below. The scale cracked upon impact, then cracked some more as it landed on the counter. The shattering sound echoed through the studio apartment. It reached the hallway and the neighbors' homes as well.

Cindy leaned back against the wall behind her. She put her palm against her forehead and wept hysterically while staring at the sparkling glass in the sink. A disturbing thought crept into her mind.

Kill yourself, the little voice said. *You can leave this crappy place. Stop the pain forever. End your miserable existence.*

She looked down at her wrist. She couldn't tell if her arm was shaking or if the tears in her eyes were making her vision jiggle.

"O–Okay," she croaked out.

She teetered forward and reached into the sink.

Her hand trembled as her fingertips touched a shard of glass. *No, it's not sharp enough*, she told herself. She pushed it aside and touched another piece. *Too small*, she thought. She kept pushing the glass, stirring it around like ingredients in a pot of soup. She was trying to buy time, hoping a positive thought would pop into her head and stop her from making a dangerous decision.

Just do it already! The little voice in her head grew louder instead.

"I'm doing it," Cindy cried out.

Her hand stopped on a large shard with a jagged, sawtooth edge. She rolled her right sleeve up and stretched her left sleeve down over her hand so it could act like a glove. She picked up the shard in her left hand. She held the spiky edge over her right wrist. She was shaking so badly that the glass nicked her, causing her to flinch.

Sniffling, she repeated, "I'm doing it."

She pressed the shard against her wrist, about an inch away from the base of her palm. It dented her flesh, then her skin *popped* like a pimple, but blood oozed out instead of pus. It leaked across her palm, then dripped off the webbing between her fingers. She whimpered as she dragged the shard across her wrist. She slit it horizontally. It was a thin two-and-a-half-inch cut.

From her wrist, hot stabs of pain shot across her arm. Her heart pounded away at her sternum, moving faster than ever before. The sight of blood and the cut, although narrow and shallow, were nauseating. Yet, she didn't feel like she was dying—not even close.

Deeper! The voice in her head roared.

"I'm trying," Cindy said feebly.

With a little more pressure, she cut into her wrist right below the first laceration. This time, she *sawed* into her skin. More blood raced out, heavy drops *plopping* on the broken glass in the sink. The bloodied glass glittered like cathedral windows in a church.

Cindy hissed in pain, spittle spurting out from between her clenched teeth. Crumbs of glass had broken off the shard. The fragments sparkled in the cut, trapped in her flesh. The pain made her entire arm shake. She was woozy now, but she still didn't feel like she was at death's door.

"No, damn it, don't tell me I'm too fat to slit my wrists," Cindy cried. "Just let me die already."

She pushed the shard against her wrist for the third time. The glass dimpled her flesh, then cut her skin again. But before she could start sawing, she heard a raspy growl. She froze with the glass buried in her wrist. Following the noise, she turned her head slowly until her eyes settled on the bathroom doorway. She could only see the kitchen.

The front door was locked, her apartment was on the fourth floor, and pets weren't allowed in the building. The noise couldn't have come from an animal— and that terrified her.

She turned her whole body to face the doorway. She heard more growling, then a footstep. She took two steps back.

In a guttural voice, a woman sang: ♪ *Side to side, death is denied. Up and down, death is around.*

Cindy reached for her pockets and looked at the bathroom counter. Her cell phone was nowhere in sight. She heard more footsteps.

The woman repeated: ♪ *Side to side, death is denied. Up and down, death is around.*

Cindy tried to run forward, but she felt like her feet were encased in buckets of cement. A paralyzing fear grabbed her.

"Help!" she yelled. "Help! There's someone in my apartment! Help me!"

Her eyes widened with alarm as a scrawny woman stepped into the bathroom doorway. Curly gray hair stuck out of her head, pointing every which way. There was a cadaverous pallor to her haggard face. Her eyes were milky and glassy. She was nude, blue and green veins standing out against her pale, thin skin. Her body was spotted with what appeared to be blue and purple bruises. Unlike her head, her crotch was hairless.

Under her small, sagging breasts, Cindy could see the woman's protuberant ribs. She looked like she was completely lacking any fat or muscle.

The intruder sang: ♪ *Side to side, death is denied. Up and down, death is around.*

Cindy saw her brown decaying teeth, bloody gums,

and yellow tongue. Her eyes were drawn to the shard of glass in the woman's left hand. It had a similar serrated edge and it was bloody as well.

"You," Cindy squeaked out, awed. "You're the woman from the theater. How did you... How did you get in my apartment?"

The intruder raised her left arm and pointed at Cindy with the shard. Her arm swayed and vibrated, as if she were carrying a heavy dumbbell in her hand.

Cindy took another step back and said, "The police are coming. I have a burglar alarm system. It's a–a *silent* alarm." She was lying, and she couldn't even believe it herself. Raising her voice, she said, "My neighbor's a cop. If I scream again, he'll–"

The intruder growled as she barreled into the bathroom. Cindy screamed and stumbled back. She crashed into the wall behind her, bending the towel rack. She grabbed onto the toilet's tank to stop herself from collapsing and put her right hand up to her face —palm facing away from her—to protect herself.

The intruder swung the shard at Cindy, slicing her wrist and completing the third self-inflicted laceration. The gash was a little longer and a little deeper than the others. With another swing, the glass ate away at her wrist again. Closing in on the center of her forearm, the fourth cut was parallel to the others.

"Stop! Stop it, *please!*" Cindy wept.

The glass sliced her again. She heard her skin tear like paper and the shard crackle as fragments crumbled off it. The fifth gash was diagonal, cutting through the other four, like a cluster of tally marks on a prison wall.

With her eyes closed, Cindy swung her arm at the woman to try to push her away. She missed her attacker, swinging at the air instead—*whoosh!* Blood from her slit wrist hit the shower curtain and the wall in a drizzle. She lost her footing and fell to the floor between the bathtub and the toilet.

"No! Oh my God, no!" she yelled as she felt her pants sliding down.

She opened her eyes to a squint, then shut them and screamed again. The intruder was crouching over her legs while tugging on her pants. Cindy crossed her arms over her face to protect herself and swung her legs wildly in an attempt to fight back. But once again, she missed every swing.

Questions flooded Cindy's bewildered mind: *How did this woman get in here? Why is she attacking me? Do I know her? Is she going to kill me? How is she so skinny and so strong? Am I dying?*

Cindy's bare thigh was sliced two times, then twice more, then two more times. Her other thigh was sliced in the same pattern. The cuts were thin but painful. Drops of blood ran down her thighs.

"Stop!" Cindy barked.

She heard three loud *thuds* behind her and then a muffled voice. It was her annoyed neighbor. She lowered her arms cautiously and cracked an eye open.

The intruder was gone. Blood was smeared on the tile floor in front of her, but there were no footprints in the room. She looked down at her lap. Three Xs were cut into each thigh. She was holding the shard of glass in her left hand. It had torn through her sleeve and sliced her palm.

"What... What happened?" she mumbled.

She grabbed the towel from the rack above her and used it to wipe the blood off her thighs and arms. She got up to her feet and pulled her pants up. She was more concerned about the intruder than she was about her wounds. She grabbed a hand towel from near the sink and tied it around her mangled wrist to slow the bleeding. She wrapped another small towel around her cut hand, then limped to the doorway.

At first, she thought about locking herself in the bathroom. It didn't seem wise to corner herself, though. She moved to the front door. As she reached for the doorknob and deadbolt, she noticed two things—the chain lock was secured, so the apartment had been locked from the inside, and she only heard the television behind her.

She's still in here, she thought. *Or she was never here to begin with.*

She turned around and looked at every corner of her apartment. She checked every cupboard in the kitchen, then she looked inside the closet and under the bed. She checked behind the curtain over her window, too. Then she looked up, as if she were expecting to find the intruder crawling across her ceiling like a spider.

The woman had vanished into thin air.

Cindy muted the television, then sat on her bed. She craned her neck forward and moved her head from side to side, her eyes cycling between the front door and the window. They were the only possible entrances in the apartment, and she kept watching them for five minutes. The intruder didn't return. She didn't hear any growling, either.

She took her cell phone off the nightstand and thought about calling Joseph or Charlotte or the police. But she couldn't unlock her phone because of the blood on her fingers. *It's better that way,* she told herself. *What was I going to tell them? A crazy woman appeared in my apartment, attacked me, then disappeared?* It sounded absurd to her—and she experienced it.

She curled into a ball on her bed and stared at the front door, holding her cell phone tight in her hand —*just in case*. She replayed the attack over and over in her head.

"What's happening to me?" Cindy sobbed as she buried her face in her pillow.

4

THE LUNCH DATE

ALTHOUGH SHE KEPT HER EYES CLOSED, CINDY MOANED as she awoke to a buzzing noise. She felt like there was a roaring chainsaw next to her head. Then she heard music—*Confident* by Demi Lovato—and more buzzing. It took her a few seconds to realize it was her ringtone. Her eyes fluttered open and she moaned again.

She rolled onto her back, then sat up in bed and glanced around. The towel wrapped around her hand had come undone during her sleep. There was a bloody handprint on her pillow. The blood drizzled on her bedsheets, comforter, and headboard had dried. She cringed as she looked at the gash on her palm. The cut was thin, but the blood made it look much worse.

The other towel was still wrapped around her sliced forearm. A disquieting tingling sensation surrounded the stinging cuts on her wrist. *Oh no,* she thought. *Some type of nerve damage? Do I have to go to the hospital?* As she moved to sit on the side of the bed, she felt the burning pain on her thighs and saw the blotches of blood on her pants.

The phone stopped ringing.

Cindy moved her comforter, then her pillow. She found the bloodied towel wedged between the mattress and the headboard. She wrapped it around her wounded hand again. She looked at the tub of ice cream on the floor. The ice cream had melted and left a large white stain with brown streaks of peanut butter on the carpet.

Her eyes narrowed as she glanced at the window in front of her. Bright columns of sunshine entered her apartment through the gaps between her curtains. Morning had arrived to pluck her from her dreams and drop her into her real-life nightmare.

As she reached for her cell phone to check the time, the device vibrated and the ringtone played again. The default photo of a person's silhouette appeared on the incoming call screen. The caller ID read: *Peter R.*

"Shit," Cindy muttered. She sighed, swiped her finger across the screen, then held the phone up to her ear and said, "Peter, I was *just* about to call you."

"Where are you, Cindy?" Peter replied with a cold voice.

"Well, that's what I was going to call you about. I'm... home."

"*Home?* You were supposed to clock in over *thirty*

minutes ago. Tell me you just went back because you forgot your phone or your keys or something."

"No, I... I can't come in today. I'm sorry. I had a–"

"Ah, what the hell, Cindy? I need you here answering phones. You know how it is with this damn strike. We can't keep losing people. I thought we were on the same page. I thought you were on our side."

Cindy worked as a customer service representative for a telecommunications company. Her coworkers marched for higher wages and better working conditions. Although she agreed with them, she decided to support her superiors and continue working in hopes of receiving preferential treatment once the strike was resolved. She wanted to be on the winning side, and she figured she couldn't lose if she minded her own business and acted like everything was normal.

If the strike was successful, all of the employees would benefit. If the strike was a failure, her bosses would appreciate her support.

"I'm on your side," she said. "I get it. I totally get it. But I had an accident."

"What kind of accident?"

"I cut my hand on some broken glass. I think–"

"Can you still come in?" Peter interrupted, unemotional. "You can still use a keyboard and a headset, can't you?"

Cindy thought about saying yes and hurrying to the office to earn some sweet brownie points. But then she noticed the tingle in her cut hand. Her stress spiked.

She said, "No. My palm is cut up real bad and I have some small cuts on my fingers. I might need stitches."

"If you go get stitches now, you think you can come in for an afternoon shift?"

Cindy rolled her eyes and shook her head. There was a mix of desperation and frustration in Peter's voice. He had trouble taking no for an answer.

"Can I call you later?" Cindy asked.

Peter blew out a loud exhale of annoyance, then said, "Yeah, yeah. Call me as soon as you're available. And whatever you do, do *not* talk to anyone in the strike. I don't want to see you around Hector or Joe. I don't care if Joe tries to play nice with you. Those greedy pricks are two testicles in the same sweaty sack. They're just trying to fuck us over. Don't forget that."

Cindy stayed quiet during his rant. She wasn't shocked by his vulgar insults, though. She had heard his abusive language before. She was just more concerned about her problems than Peter's.

She said, "I won't."

"Good. *Call me.*"

The call ended abruptly. Cindy lowered the phone to her lap and stared at the screen. The clock read: *11:35 AM*. Her physical pain and depression had put her to sleep for nearly twelve hours. She had recently been limiting her sleep to seven hours and thirty minutes.

According to another one of her favorite social media health gurus, it was the perfect amount of sleep. She enjoyed waking up at sunrise to avoid the crowds at the gym, too.

"It's probably packed now," she murmured.

She put her phone on the nightstand, then walked to the bathroom. Her lips drooped into a frown as she surveyed the mess—blood and glass everywhere. She didn't have the energy to clean it up. She ran warm water in the sink, soaked a fresh towel, then wrung it out. She pulled her pants down, then used the wet towel to clean her cuts. After drying herself, she plastered extra-large Band-Aid patches over all the cuts. To finish up, she wrapped one elastic bandage around her hand and another around her forearm.

Joseph had given her the elastic bandages after she tripped and sprained her ankle while stepping off a curb. The bandages weren't meant to treat cuts, but she made do with them.

After patching herself up, she exited the bathroom. She thought about the intruder she had encountered during the previous night. She checked the locks on the door again. *You're safe, Cin,* she told herself. She went back to her bed and flipped her pillow over so she didn't have to see her blood. The mere act of closing her eyes filled her with a sense of satisfaction. Her room vanished, replaced with the red darkness from the sunshine hitting her closed eyelids. She felt like she was resting on a cloud, floating away from her troubles on a cool night.

She fell asleep.

A *buzzing* sound awoke her again. She heard the ending of her ringtone.

"Peter," she groaned.

She rolled over and took her phone off the night-stand. The clock read: *12:13 PM*. She had received three text messages and she missed one call from Charlotte.

The messages read:

You didn't call last night. You off today??
Wanna grab lunch or coffee? Call me, okay?
Nvm, I'll call you.

The last text message ended with a smiling face emoji and a heart emoji. A smile crept onto Cindy's face as she thought about Charlotte's childlike purity. She had planned on shutting herself away for the day, but she couldn't resist her friend's invitation. She called her back. Her little smile grew into a full grin as she listened to the ringback tone.

"Cin?" Charlotte answered wonderingly.

"Hey, Charlotte. Sorry I missed your messages. How are you?"

"Don't worry about it, hon. I thought you might be

at work. Oh, you're not at work, are you? Is this a bad time?"

"No, no, it's fine. I was, um... I'm off today. I had a 'small' accident with some broken glass, so I'm just taking a 'me day.'"

"Oh no. Was it bad? You going to be all right?"

Cindy put her bandaged hand over her mouth and snickered. She was overjoyed to hear the genuine concern in Charlotte's voice. She felt like she was being coddled by her mother.

She said, "I'll be fine. I'm already patched up and good to go."

"Then what do you say we go out for coffee?"

"Now?"

"Yeah, now. Are you free? There's this new café close to your place. It's called Henry's Coffee. I've been dying to try it. What do you say?"

Say no, Cindy told herself as she looked at her bandaged wrist. *How are you going to explain this to her?* She knew Charlotte was a perceptive woman, so she couldn't hide the truth from her. She glanced back at the front door. She heard the building's usual groaning and creaking. It reminded her of the intruder's growl. She feared the mysterious woman more than Charlotte's disapproval.

"You still there?" Charlotte asked.

"Yeah," Cindy replied. "Just wondering if I was forgetting to do something. But no, it was nothing. I'm free. Let's meet."

"Perfect. Henry's Coffee, okay? Don't get it confused with Harry's Café. *Henry's Coffee*. It's close, I promise. I'll be there in about half an hour."

"It might take me a *little* longer than that to get ready."

"Don't worry about it. Take your time. You know I always have a book to keep me company. See you soon, okay?"

"Yeah, see you soon."

The call disconnected. She put the phone down on the nightstand and sat in silence for a minute. Staring at her injuries, she thought: *How do I hide this?* She hurried to her closet while trying to think up some excuses.

Cindy sat across from Charlotte with a stiff, unconvincing smile on her tight face. She held a mug filled with piping hot coffee in her right hand. The weight of the drink aggravated the cuts on her wrist, but she played it off to keep a semblance of normality. She had tried to hide the injuries on her forearm under the sleeve of her sweater, but only ten minutes into their meeting, a piece of the elastic bandage had slipped out. The gash on her palm was easy to explain so she didn't bother to hide it, but the wounds on her wrist were difficult to excuse.

There was a round table between them with Charlotte's mug and her book—*Carrie* by Stephen King—as well as both of their cell phones on top. Around them, the other patrons chattered, sipped coffee, ate baked goods, read books, and wrote manuscripts and screenplays.

Charlotte sat with a frown and a set of downcast eyes. She hadn't said a word since Cindy explained her injuries—*'I broke a glass, then slipped and fell on the shards.'*—two minutes earlier. Cindy was expecting Charlotte to be disappointed and upset. Instead, she only found great concern on her face. Charlotte had never dealt with suicide before. Although she wanted to help—her inner voice was telling her to reach over and grab Cindy in a bear hug—she was scared of saying the wrong thing and terrified of losing her close friend.

In an understanding tone, she asked, "What can I do for you?"

"Wha–What do you mean?" Cindy stuttered, her smile wavering. "I told you, I'm fine. It should heal up on its own. I'll probably go to the doctor later just to be safe, though."

Charlotte said, "I'm talking about your..." Her voice faded on the last word. She looked around, then leaned forward with her elbows on the table. She asked, "Do you want to talk about this somewhere else?"

'Yes.' Cindy choked on that word. She wanted to say it so badly, but it just wouldn't come out. She grunted,

then chuckled instead. She was in total denial, unable to ask for help or retreat from the conversation.

She said, "I'm fine here. The coffee's great, isn't it? So, um... What's on your mind?"

"Well, if you're okay, if you feel safe and comfortable, why don't you tell me what's on *your* mind, hon?"

Tell that bitch to mind her own business, the little voice in Cindy's head said. She responded with a one-syllable laugh—*Ha!*—to stop herself from following her inner voice's advice. Her shoulders hitched up to her ears and she started blinking rapidly. The coffee splashed in her mug as her trembling worsened. She was close to breaking down, close to snapping, close to saying something she was sure she was going to regret.

Charlotte reached over and grabbed her hand. Cindy drew a short gasp. She stopped shaking and her shoulders slackened. A comfortable warmth and a feeling of calm spread through her.

Her magic touch, she thought as a real smile played about the corners of her mouth.

"Talk to me, Cin," Charlotte said.

Cindy nodded as she set her mug down. She glanced around, taking a moment to think about what she was going to say. She didn't want to say too much because she was afraid the hard truth would alarm her friend, but she wanted to say just enough to relieve some of her pain and stress. *Get it off your chest,* she told herself. *Don't think about anyone else. You're safe with her.*

She said, "I've been having some... 'personal' issues recently. And by recently, I mean for most of my life." She gave another insincere chuckle, then said, "You're right. You're always right. This wasn't an accident. Well, some of it was an accident. I didn't mean to cut my hand like this, y'know, but... I guess it doesn't matter. You were right."

Cindy took a moment to breathe and check her surroundings. The other patrons continued chatting and typing. Charlotte remained quiet. Her heart told her that it was her time to listen.

Just above a whisper, Cindy said, "Last night, I was feeling very sad and very lonely and very angry. Angry at myself, angry at everyone around me, angry at the world. I ended up going into the bathroom, grabbing that expensive scale I bought—the one I posted on Instagram a few months ago, remember?—and I threw it at the mirror. I didn't want to deal with those numbers anymore and I just didn't want to see myself anymore. I was tired of all of the... the bullshit."

Charlotte's eyes were wet and she was snuffling. She held a napkin up to her nose and rubbed Cindy's hand to try to comfort her. She knew what she was going to say next.

Cindy's throat was tight. She didn't have any water, so she choked down the obstruction in her throat with a swig of coffee.

She said, "I was so tired of the bullshit that I was ready to..."

The lump of anxiety rose in her throat again. She took another sip of coffee to force it down, but it kept bobbling around in her throat.

She licked her lips to moisten them, then said, "I was ready to end it. I put a shard of glass up to my wrist and I..." Her voice getting quieter with each word, she said, "I thought... about... about killing... myself."

A lengthy, whistly breath blew past her lips as she leaned back in her seat. The heavy feeling in her chest softened and the little voice in her head weakened to a garble of noise, like static on a radio. She cried inaudibly and Charlotte joined her. Some of the other customers looked their way, then they returned to their own business. Unless there were weapons or loud noises involved, most people didn't care about what others were doing in public.

"I'm sorry," Charlotte said.

"You have nothing to be sorry about."

"I do. I knew you were in pain. Even if it was only, like, subconsciously, I *knew* something was wrong, but I didn't do anything to help. I'm so sorry. And I don't know if it's the right thing to say right now, but I have to say it: I'm so fucking glad you didn't go through with it. I love you, Cin."

Blushing, Cindy said, "Love ya, too."

"I'm serious, hon. I've known you longer than I've even known myself. I don't know if that makes sense, but it's true. You're my best friend. You're important to my life and to so many people. If... If you feel bad because of anything I might have said or done, I hope you know that I'd never–"

"It wasn't because of you," Cindy interrupted. "Of course not. You're not part of that 'bullshit' I was talking about earlier. I'm just... depressed. I hate myself more than anything else in the world because of my weight. And it doesn't help that people—*society*—took away every bit of confidence I ever had. It's hard to overcome all of that. It's *very* hard."

"There are options, Cindy. Antidepressants. Therapy. And if this is about your weight, you can lose it. I know it's not easy, but it is possible. Hell, I can help you come up with a diet and exercise routine if you want me to. I'll even help you stick to it."

"Diets don't work for me. I can stop myself from eating all day and I still won't lose any weight."

"You need a diet that works for *you* and a solid exercise plan. If you follow it for a few months, I'm positive you'll shed some pounds. It won't happen overnight, but it *can* happen with some hard work. And how about this: After we get a diet going, I can sign up at your gym and we can go together. We can be gym buddies and do this together. You don't have to fight alone, hon."

Cindy saw the sincerity and kindness in Charlotte's eyes. *What did I do to get a friend like her?* she thought.

She said, "Thank you for everything, Charlotte. I'm not sure you know what you'd be getting yourself into, though. You're probably better off getting as far away from me as possible. I'm a... a ticking time bomb."

"Then I guess I'm part of the bomb squad, huh?"

Cindy laughed, then said, "I'm serious. When I say it's hard, I mean it's *hard*. Depression—*real* depression—is like poison. It's like... like your mind is trying to force your body to self-destruct but your heart keeps fighting. It stops you from doing the things you want to do and makes you do things you normally wouldn't do. And once it's in you... I don't think you can ever really get it out of your system."

"I understand. I might not be going through it, but I get it. I'll be by your side as long as you let me stand by you. And when you need time for yourself, I'll back off and let you breathe. That can work, right?"

Cindy had trouble accepting Charlotte's offer. The little voice in her head was getting louder. *You'd be a burden,* it said. *You don't want to be her burden, do you? How long can she carry your fat body before you crush her?* She responded with a tight-lipped smile and a slight nod.

Charlotte said, "And if you ever feel like you're not getting the results you want, you can always consider surgery or diet pills, right? I'm not talking, like, liposuction or anything like that, but there are surgeries that make your stomach smaller so you'll eat less. And I've heard some pills suppress your appetite. My mom used to take 'em. It might be worth looking into, huh?"

"I guess it wouldn't hurt to look into it. I'll keep

trying to exercise and diet in the meantime. Not much else I can do right now."

"Whatever you decide to do, I'm here."

"Thank you. Really, thank you for everything."

They continued their chat while drinking their coffee. They spoke about exercise and diets for a few minutes, then their conversation moved on to other topics: Work, relationships, movies. Cindy stayed as attentive as possible, often focusing on Charlotte's mouth as if she were trying to read her lips. Yet, throughout the rest of their meeting, the little voice lingered at the back of her mind.

We'll get you next time, it said.

5

BACK TO THE GYM

"Baby steps, Cin, baby steps," Cindy whispered. "You don't have to run to the finish line to finish the race. You can walk out of this. You can do this."

All around her, dumbbells and weight plates clicked and clanked. Treadmills rumbled and ellipticals whirred. Weightlifters groaned with each rep as they pumped iron in front of the mirrors. Some of them screamed and slammed their weights, as if they wanted *everyone* to look at them. Most of the guests listened to music and podcasts and audiobooks during their exercises. A few people spoke—gym partners, guys trying to pick up girls, employees pestering customers about personal training programs—but their voices were drowned out by the gym's pop music.

Ultimately, everyone in the gym minded their own business.

Cindy was taking a brisk walk on a treadmill at the

far end of the gym. Beads of sweat shimmered on her red face and neck. The sweat drenched her long-sleeve shirt and yoga pants, too. She looked like she had jumped into a pool without undressing thirty minutes earlier. Her eyes were fixed on the treadmill's calories burned counter. The number increased every few seconds—*132... 133... 134*. She knew it wasn't entirely accurate, but it helped her keep track of her goals. If the number surpassed her previous record, then her exercise was a success.

She turned her attention to the mirror in front of the treadmill. She saw the human blob staring back at her, but it appeared a *little* smaller. She still felt fat, but she no longer saw herself as a complete slob—as a horrendous monster. A flicker of optimism sparked in her chest. The only voices in her head were her own and Charlotte's. *You can lose it,* she remembered Charlotte saying. A smile tugged on her lips, but she wrestled it away.

Positivity, optimism, and self-love were limited resources in her life. She hoped to bottle it up and save it for later.

She stopped the treadmill and wiped the sweat off her face with a small towel. While chugging her water, she glanced around the gym. The afternoon rush hour hadn't started yet. Fueled by her newfound confidence, she decided to fit one more exercise into her schedule.

"Something easy, something where I can sit," she murmured.

Like a boxer dodging jabs, she weaved and bobbed her head to peek around the gym equipment and other guests. Her gaze stopped on a row of stationary bikes near the front desk. She made her way over to the equipment, shuddering with a mix of nervousness and excitement. It was her first time using a stationary bike. She was scared of breaking it while simultaneously feeling like she was taking a huge step forward for her health.

Someone crashed into her as she bent over to put her water bottle on the floor next to the bike. Wobbling, she grabbed onto the bike's seat to keep her balance. She saw the other person's bottle bouncing on the floor and heard the pink beverage sloshing inside of it. A towel landed between two stationary bikes. As she steadied herself, she took two steps back, hung her head, and stayed quiet.

Act natural, she told herself. *Grab the bottle, give it back to them, and apologize. This is your chance to be normal.*

The other person grabbed the towel first. Cindy lunged at the bottle and, just as she grabbed it, the other person touched it, too. It was a man. She jerked her hand away, took another step back, and cast her eyes at the floor.

"Sorry about that," the man said. "You okay?"

Cindy answered with a barely perceptible nod. She hoped it was enough to end the encounter.

The man asked, "I didn't hurt you, did I?"

His voice, although deep and masculine, reminded her of Charlotte's. There was a genuine tenderness to it. She looked at him so she could answer him, but her quick glance turned into a long, captivated gaze. She didn't recognize him, but she felt comfortable in his presence. She was attracted to him.

His straight black hair was combed over. There was stubble on his chin and upper lip. His eyes were like honey, brown and sweet. He wore a sleeveless black shirt, revealing his toned, muscular arms.

"I–I'm sorry," Cindy stuttered. "I should have been watching where I was going. I was, um... I guess I was a little dizzy."

"You kidding?" the man said, smiling. "*I* bumped into *you*. I should have been more careful. You sure you okay? You said you were dizzy. You wanna sit down?"

"Oh, I'm okay now, really. Like, totally okay," Cindy said with an awkward laugh.

"All right. I'll get out of your hair then. Have a good one."

The guy squeezed past Cindy in what felt like slow motion. *Say something!* she yelled at herself. Meanwhile, the little voice in her head—weak from a lack of speaking recently—said: *Don't... fool... yourself. He'll... hurt... you. He'll... hate... you.*

"My name's Cindy," she blurted out. The man looked back at her. Cindy asked, "What's yours? I mean, if you don't mind me asking."

The man narrowed his eyes and smiled at her. She

looked uncomfortable, jittery and tired, so he wasn't expecting her to continue the conversation.

He said, "Hideki. My friends call me Deki, though, and my patients call me Dr. Deki."

"Doctor? You mean like a *real* doctor? Or is that some sort of pick-up line?"

"I guess it's a little of both."

Oh my God, Cindy thought. *That means he's really trying to flirt with me.* She heard faint rumblings from the little voice at the back of her head. Her happiness and confidence were smothering it. Although she had stopped exercising, her cheeks brightened and her heart sped up.

"Really?" she said. "So, um... What kind of doctor are you, Dr. Deki? What do you practice?"

"It's a little difficult to explain."

"Why?"

"Well, let me put it this way: I make people beautiful."

"You mean like a plastic surgeon?"

Deki wiped the sweat off the nape of his neck with his towel and moved closer to Cindy. She felt like he was moving in for a kiss, his breath caressing her sweaty face with each exhale.

Lowering his voice but speaking loud enough so she could hear him over the music, he said, "No, no. I don't operate. I have my own ways, my own techniques, my own... medicine." He caressed her cheek and said, "You know, you'd be absolutely gorgeous,

I'm talking drop-dead *stunning*, if you lost some weight."

Cindy's head swung back, as if the man had punched her in the face. Her confidence crumbled, sending shockwaves through her body. *I told you so!* the little voice roared in her head.

"Eh–Excuse me?" she said.

"Shit," Deki responded, eyes growing with alarm. "That's not how I meant it. I'm so sorry."

"It's... fine. I should just... I have to get going."

"Wait. Please, just wait a second. Can I explain?"

Cindy was hurt, but there was something about Deki that she couldn't resist. She crossed her arms, pouted, and nodded at him, as if to say: '*Go ahead, but tread lightly.*'

"What I meant to say was: I can see your *true* potential. I make people beautiful, so I know beautiful people —and *you*, Cindy, are beautiful. I'll be honest, I've seen you around here before. You're doing great. And your results are only going to get better over time. I know it."

"And how do you know that?"

"Because you're a fighter. Because you're still trying to improve. Because I can help you... if you're interested."

Cindy was suspicious of his motives. She had never seen him at the gym before. Then again, she tended to keep her head down when she was out in public.

She asked, "What are you talking about?"

"Can you step outside with me for a minute?"

Cindy's eyes, wide and alarmed, darted to the front desk. Deki could see the shout for help building up in her neck.

He smiled, waved both of his hands, and said, "I'm not asking you to follow me to an alley or into a windowless van. Nothing like that. I'm talking, like, right in front of the entrance. Just somewhere where we can get away from the eavesdroppers. We could both use the fresh air anyway, don't you think?"

Cindy was getting more uncomfortable by the minute. She was curious, though, and she didn't feel like she was in any immediate danger. As a matter of fact, she convinced herself that she would feel safer if she was closer to her car, which was parked right in front of the gym. She nodded, then followed him out. They loitered near the entrance.

Deki said, "I'll try to get straight to the point. I produce and distribute a special capsule—*my medicine*. This capsule helps the 'patient' lose an *enormous* amount of weight without exercising or dieting. In fact, while using these capsules, it is recommended to continue eating as you regularly would. These things eat fat faster than you can possibly imagine. It will *really* eat into you if you're not careful. But it gets the job done."

"Are you kidding me?"

"I am one hundred percent serious. I wouldn't be

telling you about this if I didn't think it would help you. It's sort of a secret."

"And that's why you asked me to come out here with you? I'm sorry, but this sounds sketchy. Miracle weight loss pills? Seriously?"

"*Capsules.*"

"Okay. Miracle weight loss *capsules*? You think I haven't heard that one before? You're not a doctor. You're probably part of some pyramid scheme. Just a salesman, right? A scammer?"

Deki said, "I can prove it to you. Turn around and look inside the gym. There's a girl on the StairMaster. She used to weigh about 250 pounds. I sold her some capsules and now look at her. She lost the fat and kept her curves. If you don't believe me, you can go ask her yourself."

Cindy peered into the gym. She saw a brunette with a shapely figure—the type she admired—on a StairMaster. *Is he bluffing?* she thought. *Does he know I'm too nervous to go in there and ask her?* She looked back at Deki. He had an air of confidence about him that made every word out of his mouth sound like indisputable fact.

"What kind of capsules are we talking here? What do they do? How much do they cost? You're not really selling 'em to me."

Deki said, "In layman's terms, they're diet capsules. The 'medicine' inside eats your fat. I mean that in an almost *literal* sense. It'll start slow, but it will accelerate over time. The 'medicine' will spread and settle in your body."

"Medicine... You keep emphasizing that word. Why?"

"It's technically not medicine. It's difficult to explain. But it's safe. Just remember to only take *two* capsules per week. Preferably on a Thursday and Sunday to spread it out a little. And it's important to eat as much as possible. Forget about calorie counting. Just eat. That's all you have to do."

With hesitation in her voice, Cindy said, "That sounds... counter-productive."

"It's for your own safety, Cindy. Like I said, it *eats* your fat. When there's no more fat to eat, it can move on to the rest of your body. And when it does that, your body and your mind will force you to adapt. That means you may be convinced into eating... things you've never thought about eating before. In other words, you'd develop some really bad appetites. You get me? Eat until your losing weight at a comfortable rate. That's all you have to worry about."

"Let's say I believe you. I believe in your miracle 'capsules.' How much does it cost?"

Deki unzipped his backpack and pulled an orange prescription bottle out. He pushed down on it, then twisted the cap until it came off. He leaned closer to Cindy and showed her the bottle. The container held 30 size-1 capsules, each one approximately one-and-a-half centimeters in length. Each capsule was half white and half red—*blood red*.

As he screwed the cap back on, Deki said, "It's $1,000 for a 30-capsule prescription. That should last you over three months. You'll see impressive results in half that time. I don't sell them indivi–"

"That's, like, thirty bucks per capsule," Cindy interrupted. "That's crazy."

"Well, I usually sell these to *severely* obese people. I'm talking 400, 500, 600 pounds and up. You won't need all of these capsules, but like I was saying, I don't sell them individually. It's against my policy and I don't break my policy for anyone."

There was a moment of quiet as they thought about the business transaction. A woman left the gym while two guys arrived.

Deki said, "You're looking for a miracle and I have that for you. I have it for you in one of these clean, orange bottles. Give it four weeks, eight capsules, and you'll lose all of that fat. Then, if you'd like, you can sell the rest or save them. You probably know someone who could use a miracle, too, and remember, this isn't a permanent solution, so it's your responsibility to keep that weight off."

Cindy immediately thought about Joseph. She figured he could use the capsules with her and they could split the cost.

She said, "You're talking like you've already sold them to me."

"That's because I have. I can see it in your eyes."

Cindy frowned and stared down at herself, ashamed. Deki was right. He was a master salesman. Using his charm and confidence, he sold dreams to people stuck in never-ending nightmares. Even though it sounded like it was too good to be true, Cindy was genuinely interested in the 'miracle' capsules. She had spent four years trying to lose weight—and she only ended up gaining more weight in the process. She didn't mind spending four weeks with Deki's 'medicine.' She knew she looked foolish, but she was desperate, depressed, and naïve.

"How do I know you won't scam me?" she asked. "Why should I trust you—a complete stranger—with so much money?"

Deki puckered his lips and nodded, then said, "I like you. And it's not just because you're beautiful." Cindy huffed and rolled her eyes. She had to bite her lip to stop herself from smiling. She liked his flirtatious behavior. Deki continued, "It's because you're a good person. I can see that in your eyes, too. So, I think we can work something out."

"Like what?"

"One, you can pay half today and half when you see results. So, I'd say you can pay the rest in a week or two. That's a deal you don't want to miss, especially since I don't normally do this. Two, I'll give you my personal number so you can call me anytime. And, lastly, you can trust me because I work *here*."

"What?" Cindy asked in disbelief.

Smirking, Deki reached into his backpack and pulled an employee ID badge out. The plastic card had a picture of himself, his full name, a barcode, and the gym's logo. Under his name, a line read: *PERSONAL TRAINER*. Cindy glanced over her shoulder at the man working at the front desk. An identical badge hung from his neck.

Smiling nervously, Cindy said, "I must have missed you all this time..."

"You can trust me. I'm only trying to help you out. Yes, it's an expensive supplement, but it is very effective. It's not like that other shit you've seen in those pyramid schemes. This is the real deal. So, talk to me. What are you thinking? You ready to lose that weight? Ready to find the real you in there?"

Cindy gazed into Deki's bright eyes. She could almost make out the dollar signs sparkling across his irises. He was obviously more interested in making a sale, but he seemed sincere about the capsule's abilities. She looked down at her stomach and counted the rolls of fat on her shirt. She was willing to do anything to get rid of them.

She said, "I need to go to the bank next door and withdraw some money. We..." Her voice broke and tears trickled from her hopeful eyes. She laughed and said, "We have a deal."

"Fantastic," Deki replied. "You won't regret this. I promise. You go get the money and I'll write down some instructions and tips for you. I'll be here waiting."

"Thank you. If you're the real deal, if you can really help me, I'm going to owe you much more than $500."

"You already do. You owe me a grand," Deki said—half-joking, half-serious.

6

THE MIRACLE CAPSULE

SAME THING, DIFFERENT NIGHT, CINDY THOUGHT.

Sitting in the truck's passenger seat, she stared vacantly at the apartment building to her right. Her boyfriend sat in the driver's seat. They had just finished another date where she once again experienced acute discomfort in public. She didn't want to talk about it, but she knew Joseph cared too much about her to let it go. The same sequence of events occurred after every date. She felt like her life was a sad song and it was playing on repeat.

"The food was the bomb, right? Filled you up, hmm?" Joseph asked from the driver's seat. Cindy nodded. Joseph said, "I read seafood is really healthy. A lot of protein and a little fat. But it's 'good' fat. I mean, I don't know why, but that's what I read. Maybe we can start eating sushi for lunch instead of burgers and pizza. It'll help you with your diet, right?"

Cindy grunted and nodded, as if to say: '*Sure, whatever.*' She heard every word out of his mouth, but she didn't agree with him and she didn't want to argue with him. Her problem was that she had trouble eating in moderation. Even if seafood was proven to be healthier for her than fast food, she was afraid she would just end up gorging herself on fish, gobbling up sushi rolls like potato chips.

Joseph asked, "What's up, Cindy? Talk to me." His girlfriend remained quiet. Joseph said, "C'mon. Don't push me away. You know I always come back. What are you thinking?"

Cindy pivoted in her seat to face him. She saw the sincere concern on his face—eyes narrowed, lips pursed to the side, a bundle of creases on his forehead.

She said, "You mind if I ask you something?"

"Go for it."

"What would you say if I—by some miracle—lost a lot of weight? How would you feel about me if all of this *disgusting* fat disappeared?"

"Disgusting? I never said you were disgusting."

"That's not what I'm saying and that's not the point. I'm asking–"

"I think you're perfect the way you are, babe. I wouldn't change anything about you."

Cindy huffed, then looked away and shook her head.

"Did I say something wrong?" Joseph asked.

"Yeah."

"What?"

"You lied to me. I hate it when you lie to me."

Joseph furrowed his brow and asked, "Lied about what?"

Cindy said, "You know I'm not perfect."

"You're per–"

"Perfect to you. I know, I know. I've heard it before. It doesn't matter how many times you say it or how you say it. It's not true. I'm a slob. I'm a fat, disgusting slob. I can't stand to look at my own reflection. For crying out loud, I have to take a shower with my eyes closed so I don't have to see myself. I'm not perfect, Joseph. I'm not like the girls on TV. I'm not like those 'plus-sized' models on Instagram. Those beautiful girls with those sexy curves in all the right places... I'm not like them."

Joseph turned in his seat and caressed Cindy's cheek. Her face was misted with a blend of tears and sweat.

He said, "You're better than them. And you *are* perfect to me, Cindy. I say it because it's true. I don't care about anything else. Money, curves, *whatever*. I only care about you and how you feel. You could look like this for the rest of your life or gain a hundred or two hundred pounds, and I'd still consider myself to be the luckiest man in the world."

A smile blossomed on Cindy's face. She looked back at Joseph and nodded. She wasn't attracted to him the way she was to Deki or Michael, but she found his passion charming. The man had a big, gentle heart, and he knew how to comfort her with his words.

Cindy said, "Thank you, Joe. Thank you for everything. I'm lucky to have you in my life."

She leaned over and kissed him while stroking his jaw. As she shifted back into her seat, she heard the pill bottle in her bag rattling like a maraca.

She said, "But... Um..."

Noticing her reluctance, Joseph said, "You can tell me anything."

"Yeah, um... I'm still curious. You didn't really answer my question. How would you feel if I 'magically' lost a lot of weight? I'm talking losing all of this fat in, like, four weeks?"

"In four weeks? I'm not sure I understand the question. How much weight are we actually talking here?"

"Like I said, all of my fat. So, I don't know, let's say 150 pounds. What do you think about that?"

"A hundred and fifty pounds in four weeks? You kidding?"

"Just humor me," Cindy said. "What would you think?"

Joseph chuckled, then said, "I'd probably ask something like: How the *hell* did you do that? Then I'd kiss you and move on with our day. I'd love you just like I always have. And finally, I'd probably ask you again: How the *hell* did you lose that weight so fast? Black magic?"

While her boyfriend continued laughing, Cindy

said, "Well, you can lose a lot of weight through surgery and medicine, like... pills and... *capsules*. It's possible, I guess."

Joseph's laughter came to an abrupt stop. Her words slapped the smile off his face. They looked at each other, only the sound of their heavy breathing blowing through the interior of the truck.

"What?" Cindy asked.

"Listen, Cindy, I love you and I'm always going to have your back. I'm going to support you no matter what. You know that. I just don't want you to get your hopes up for nothing. Surgery is very expensive and very dangerous. It's seriously risky. Believe me, I've done my research. And diet pills don't work. That's just the truth. I mean, if these things could really 'burn' the fat off a person, everyone would be using them. They're usually scams—dangerous scams."

Cindy looked down at her bag, disappointed by Joseph's brutal honesty. But, at heart, she felt the same skepticism about Deki's capsules as well.

Joseph said, "I'm sorry. I didn't mean to sound like an asshole. I guess surgery and pills and all that stuff just make me a little uncomfortable." Cindy kept her head down. Joseph said, "I can't stop you from doing what you think is best, so... Listen, if you want to try something new, I'll be by your side. If you want to look into some type of surgery, I'll help you pay. As long as it's safe and you're comfortable, I'll back you up. Okay?"

Cindy wanted to tell him about the 'miracle' capsules, but she didn't want him to worry. Deki's medicine wasn't approved by the FDA. As a matter of fact, she didn't know *anything* about the capsules. Years earlier, after reading about a cannibal attack in Florida, she had read about drug dealers selling synthetic cathinones—*bath salts*—in capsule form. She wondered if she had a bottle full of bath salts in her bag. Her safety wasn't guaranteed.

Burying the truth, Cindy forced a smile onto her face and said, "Sounds good. I'm going to keep exercising and dieting, but I want to look into some other options. I'm mostly curious, I guess. But, yeah, I'll keep doing what I'm doing."

"Attagirl. That's all I'm saying. Take your time, do some research, and be careful," Joseph said. He touched Cindy's bicep and said, "Damn, babe, look at these muscles. You've been hitting the gym hard recently, haven't you? Don't think I haven't noticed. You look like you can kill someone with your bare hands. Just don't get too ripped, Cin. I wouldn't want you to hurt me by accident."

"Oh, whatever," Cindy said, giggling. "I'm going to head inside already. I'll call you tomorrow."

"All right. Good night, Cin. Love ya."

"Love you, too."

They shared another kiss, then Cindy got out of the truck. She waved at her boyfriend again as she walked to her apartment building. She stopped at the foyer and waited until Joseph drove off. As soon as the truck vanished around the corner, she frowned and shook her head. Her face ached from faking her happiness all day.

———

Depression had a presence. It was the black cloud that followed people all day and the darkness in homes that couldn't be illuminated.

Cindy despised her apartment. Every night, she stood in her doorway and stared into her home, struggling to find a reason to enter it. *Because it's your home,* she always told herself. *You're supposed to feel comfortable here.* But it wasn't true. The tiny space choked her and the impenetrable darkness—those stains of depression—frightened her.

She flicked the light switch next to the door and the kitchen light flickered on. She slammed the door behind her and locked it, then checked the locks again. She threw her bag on a kitchen counter and headed to the refrigerator, like she did every night when she got home, but she stopped before she could reach it. The orange prescription bottle rolled out of her bag. Like a ringtone, the rattling called to her.

She picked it up and leaned forward with her elbows on the counter. She examined the bottle, as if it were an ancient artifact.

She whispered, "What can you really do for me?

Hmm? Can you really 'eat' all of the fat in my body? Can you make me beautiful like everyone else? Or will you just end up disappointing me? Or will you kill me? Or will you make me kill? I don't know where you've been or what's inside of you. How did Deki make you?"

She set the bottle down next to the sink, then stepped back. She shuddered as a tingly sensation shot up her spine. She felt like someone was leering at her. Her head swiveled to the left. She gasped and staggered, her eyes bugging out. The refrigerator swayed as she crashed into it.

The bathroom door was open. A triangle of light from the kitchen entered the room. She could see the sink and the broken medicine cabinet. The light also illuminated a woman's gray, bony, buckling legs. Her toenails were long and curly, yellow and brittle. Only a silhouette of her upper body was visible in the darkness.

Cindy recognized the person's bush of curly hair, skinny limbs, and pale skin—*the Starving Woman*. But the woman didn't attack her. She just stood there and stared at Cindy.

"I'll... I'll call the police," Cindy said. "My boyfriend is outside. He–He has a gun."

The woman didn't respond.

Cindy inched forward. Her eyes went to the bedroom, then back to the bathroom, then to the front door. There was only one way out. She dashed towards the front door. She unfastened the chain lock but stopped as she twisted the deadbolt. She noticed the intruder hadn't moved. Like a mannequin, the woman stood motionless in the bathroom.

Cindy stared down at her bandaged hand. She started sobbing as awful memories swirled around in her mind. She remembered her suicide attempt and the violent attack.

"It's just me," she cried. "Everything is... is me. It can't happen again. I–I can't let it end like this. If I stay fa... fa... *fat*, I'll end up dead. I'll kill myself. I have to fight back. I have to–to do something."

She stepped into the bathroom doorway. Moving cautiously, she reached for the doorknob. The intruder stayed still.

Cindy closed the door, then returned to the kitchen sink. She opened the bottle and waggled it until two capsules fell out and bounced on the counter. She filled a glass with tap water, then set it down next to the capsules.

She said, "What are my options? I can keep going to the gym. Keep seeing zero progress. Keep eating food I don't like. I can try surgery. Spend thousands of dollars. Possibly stay fat anyway. Or I can take these capsules. They might not work. They might kill me. They might save my life." She looked at the bathroom door upon hearing the intruder's growl. She said, "Or I can... kill myself."

She brought her attention back to the capsules.

She thought about Charlotte's offer to help her lose weight, Joseph's advice, and Deki's promises.

She said, "I already spent the money. I... I might as well give it a try. If they hurt me, if they kill me, then... then maybe it's better that way. I can't keep living like this. I have to move forward or I'll be left behind."

She wiped the tears from her eyes to clear her vision, then analyzed the capsules on the counter. They were all the same, but she felt like she had to pick the right one—the lucky one. She grabbed the one with the most vibrant red cap.

She sighed shakily, then opened her mouth. She placed the big capsule at the center of her tongue, then swallowed it with a swig of water. Trembling, she looked down at the other capsule on the counter. A thought surfaced in her mind: *If I double the dosage, I'll either get rid of the fat faster or kill myself faster. Win-win.* She swallowed the other one with another gulp of water. It was just like drinking pills to alleviate a headache.

She drank another glass of water, thinking it would help the capsules dissolve in her body and accelerate the weight loss process. Fidgeting, she waited in the kitchen for three minutes to see how she would react to the capsules. She was keyed up, but that was nothing new for her.

Cindy glanced at the bathroom door again upon noticing the silence. She crept over to it. She planted her ear on the door and listened—no more growling.

She drew a deep breath, then opened it. To her utter surprise, the bathroom was empty. Once again, the intruder had vanished without a trace.

"It's over," Cindy said. She dragged her feet to her bed. The floorboards rumbled as she let herself drop onto the mattress. Curling up with a blanket, she whispered, "It's time to move forward. It's time for my... rebirth."

7

A DATE

THE PERCEPTION OF TIME DEPENDED ON THE PERSON, place, and situation, shifting on a case-by-case basis. Time tended to move at a slower pace during periods of severe stress, crisis, and depression. And time seemed to accelerate during pleasurable events and sessions of relaxation. Good days often felt shorter than the bad ones.

For Cindy, time was now moving at a breakneck speed. There were no obstacles she couldn't pass, no inner voices she couldn't silence.

Wearing a white sundress, she strolled down a beach. She held her white sandals in her right hand while swinging her arms like a child with a basket on Easter. The cool wind blew her curly hair out behind her, so she couldn't hide the big, liberated smile on her face. Problems lingered in her life, but she was sure they would fix themselves. For the first time in years, she felt confident and optimistic.

Joseph held her other hand and walked next to her. He glanced at Cindy, then looked down at himself. He wore a size XXXL black t-shirt and matching mesh shorts—the usual. They were never the type of couple to wear matching clothes when they went out on dates, but they had always had a similar casual style. They were two peas in a pod. He was starting to notice all of Cindy's changes.

Her clothing was lighter and brighter. She had curled her hair and opted for minimal makeup. She was slimmer. She was happier.

Joseph stopped in his tracks and turned Cindy towards him. Behind her, the setting sun painted the sky with every tint of red and orange.

"What is it?" Cindy asked.

Joseph hesitated. He looked at her with half his face scrunched up in confusion. She even sounded a little different to him.

He said, "I didn't want to bring this up during dinner 'cause I thought it would sound awkward, but you look... great."

Cindy cocked her head back and asked, "Why would that sound awkward?"

"Because... I mean, you look different."

"Different?"

"In a good way. You *always* look great, but you look like you're glowing right now. Does that make any sense? I don't know how to explain it. You just... You look happy."

Cindy's face went pink. She wanted to say something like: '*I know. It's because I AM happy.*'

She said, "You could have said that during dinner. I still don't see why it would sound awkward. Sounds romantic to me."

Joseph said, "Because now that I see it, I don't think I've ever really seen you happy. And if I've never seen you like this before, that means..."

I was never happy with you to begin with, Cindy thought. Joseph didn't have to say it out loud to convey his concerns. They stood in silence, small waves crashing over their feet.

Cindy said, "I love you. We love each other. That's all that matters. Come on. Let's get back to your truck."

Just as she took her first step away, Joseph gave her hand a gentle tug. She stopped and looked back at him.

He said, "I need to ask you something."

"I'm listening."

"Are you happy now–"

"I was always happy," Cindy interrupted, lying through her teeth in an attempt to end the conversation.

"Are you *happier* now because you lost some weight? It's only been, like... What? A little over a week since I've seen you? And you've changed so much. It's... It's pretty crazy."

Cindy shrugged and stared down at herself. She had lost twenty-five pounds since consuming the first set of miracle capsules eight days earlier. Before taking Deki's 'medicine,' the most she had ever lost in a week was four pounds. And back then, she couldn't tell if the weight loss was caused by natural fluctuations.

Joseph put his finger on her chin and lifted her head to look into her eyes. He said, "Look at yourself, Cin. Your face is slimmer. Your body's tighter. I'm sorry if I sound rude. I'm just amazed. I don't know what else to say."

Cindy pulled his hand away from her chin and said, "You don't have to say anything else about it. I totally get you. I'm happy. You're happy. I love you. You love me. Let's just change the subject, okay? Do you have your tuxedo ready for Charlotte's wedding? Michael's been texting me about it. He said you haven't gotten back to him yet."

"About that... I'm not going to make it to the wedding. The ceremony, the reception, none of it."

"What? Why?"

"My brother will be in town that weekend. I haven't seen him in four years. Almost five, actually. He's only going to be around that weekend, too."

"I'm sure Charlotte and Michael wouldn't mind if you brought him along."

Joseph gave a half-hearted smile and said, "I thought about it, but I don't think he wants to spend a day at a party with people he doesn't even know. He barely even knows you, Cindy. It's just bad timing, I guess. I think of Michael as a brother, too, but this is *blood* we're talking about here. My *real* brother, y'know? I'm going to pick him over a party every time. I'm sorry, babe."

"No, no, I get it," Cindy said with a hint of disappointment in her voice.

She was gaining confidence and losing weight at a rapid pace, but she wasn't sure if she was ready to attend a party by herself, especially a wedding reception. Guests always tried to look their best at weddings. Some even tried to outdo the brides and grooms. Since Joseph was much bigger than her, she was hoping he would draw all of the judgmental eyes at the party away from her.

"If I had a brother or sister, I'd probably do the same," she said. As she wandered over to the dry sand, she said, "I'll go alone. I'll stop by, say hello, wish 'em a happy marriage, then head home once things start to get uncomfortable."

The smile returned to her face as she felt the warm sand under her feet. It was unusually calming and reassuring. She looked over at the sea. Surrounded by darkness, a pillar of orange light stretched across the water—from the sun falling beyond the horizon to the shore at her feet. She continued walking to the parking lot.

Joseph jogged to catch up to her, sending clumps of wet sand through the air with each step. Then he slowed to a stroll next to her. He was about to speak, but the short run left him breathless.

After wheezing for a few seconds, he said, "Now that... that we've got that out of the way, let's talk about you. I mean, if that's okay. I don't want to pressure you or anything like that, but I still have questions."

Looking straight ahead, Cindy asked, "What is it?"

"I wanna know how you did it."

"You're still talking about the weight thing?"

"Tell me about it. Please, Cindy."

Cindy had been wanting to talk to someone about the miracle capsules since the day she bought them. She was eager to talk about her progress and her hopes for the future. But she didn't know much about Deki's medicine, so she didn't have much to say about the capsules. She only knew that the capsules were working and she was happy with the results so far.

"Do you want the truth?" she asked.

"Always."

"The truth is... I lost 25 pounds—maybe 30 by now —with a pill. Well, it's technically a *capsule*, but you know what I mean. I took two last week and another one a few days ago. I've been eating whatever I want— ice cream, cheesecake, steak, burgers, entire pizzas— and I'm still losing a couple of pounds every day. It's literally a miracle capsule, Joseph."

"You lost all of that weight with a pill?"

"Capsules, but yeah, that's right."

"And you're saying you ate whatever you wanted? Really?"

Cindy said, "I know it's hard to believe. It's hard for me to make sense of any of it. But it's the truth. This thing is eating all of my fat. It doesn't even look like I'll have that much loose skin after. It's amazing, right?"

Joseph nodded and stroked his beard while inspecting every inch of his girlfriend's figure. Her claims left him dumbfounded. He was afraid she was starving herself, but then he remembered their date earlier in the evening. They ate California Cheesesteaks with French fries and had cheesecake for dessert at the Cheesecake Factory. She didn't hesitate to eat any of it. As a matter of fact, she finished eating before he did.

One question bothered his mind: *What kind of capsule 'eats' fat while the person eats more food?* He had spent hours researching weight loss solutions, but he couldn't think of an answer.

He grunted, then said, "I think it's great and all that you're happy. You know that's all I've ever wanted for you. But... I'm a little worried. Three capsules, almost thirty pounds, plenty of eating... It doesn't make any sense. And if it's true–"

"It is," Cindy said.

"–then it *can't* be healthy. If it were, everyone would know about it and everyone would be using it. What kind of diet pill is it? What's the brand?"

Cindy didn't understand the science behind the

capsules, so she didn't know how to explain it. She couldn't even tell him a single ingredient. '*Magic.*' She choked on the word. She didn't want to alarm her boyfriend by skirting around the subject with a joke. She thought about telling him the truth: '*Oh, I just bought them from a shady but handsome guy who works at the gym.*' But she was afraid it would only unsettle him even more.

She said, "The truth is, I don't know every little thing about it. I only know that it's supposed to eat fat. That's how it was, um... advertised. It's obviously working, too. If you're, like, concerned about my health or whatever, you can stop worrying. Seriously, I'm fine. I've never felt better. My body is strong and my mind is clear. And, hey, at the first sign of trouble, I already decided I'm going to run straight to my doctor. You have my word on that, so please don't blow this out of proportion."

Joseph said, "I know you, Cindy. You'll only run to the doctor if it's not an 'embarrassing' problem. If it *is* embarrassing, you're going to ignore it."

Cindy said, "Don't be ridiculous. I'm not a child. I understand the risks. I know diet pills can be dangerous. I've read it all, too, okay? You're not the only one with the internet, Joe."

Dispirited, Joseph dropped his head and stared at the sand. He hated arguing with her. They stopped again. They could hear adults chattering and kids yelling in the nearby parking lot.

Cindy grabbed Joseph's hand and said, "Listen, hon, I took a chance with these capsules. I took the test run and I'm fine. I haven't had any problems. And you said it yourself: I look great and I'm happy. So, I want to offer you the same thing. I want to help you lose weight and be happy. Happier than ever before. Will you join me on this journey? Can we do this together?"

Joseph felt the sincerity in Cindy's voice. His insecurities grew stronger as she slimmed down, though. He questioned her intentions as pessimism opened the door to doubt in his mind. He felt like he wasn't good enough for her anymore. His cynical mind told him that what she was really asking was: *Will you lose weight with me or should I leave you for someone better?*

He said, "I don't know if I can do that. I don't even know what's in these things or where you got them."

Cindy said, "Don't think about any of that right now. All you have to do is answer one question. Do you trust me?"

"Yeah. Of course I trust you."

"Then that's all you need. Trust me and everything will be fine."

She opened her purse and pulled out a small Ziploc bag. It was filled with fifteen miracle capsules—half of her supply. She had prepared the bag before their date just in case she worked up the courage to tell him about them. She was hoping she could convince him to pay half of the bill after he saw some results as well.

She said, "If you take these, then I know you're standing with me. We'll lose weight together. We'll become healthy together. We'll become attractive together. We'll... We'll become the *perfect* couple. No more sadness. No more pain. No more bullying. I understand if you don't want to take them, but I honestly believe this will help us more than anything."

Running his fingertips across the bag, Joseph marveled at the capsules, hypnotized by their red caps. They looked like they were glowing in the dark.

He said, "I'm always with you, Cin. I'm just a little scared. That's all."

"There's nothing to be scared of. Just take the capsules, then forget about it. You can eat whatever you want. You don't even have to exercise. These capsules will handle everything. Please trust me, Joseph. I would never put you in harm's way. I want you to come on this journey with me. I don't want to do this alone. I don't want to leave you behind."

Joseph's face cramped with fear and sadness. Cindy's last sentence fueled his pessimism. *She's going to leave me if I don't lose weight like her,* he thought. He snatched the bag out of her hand, then dug his fingers into his hair and stepped back. He feared losing the love of his life more than he feared taking the mysterious capsules.

"Okay, okay," he said. "I'll join you on this 'journey' or whatever you want to call it. But I'm not going to hesitate to call 911 if anything goes wrong."

With a small smile, Cindy said, "I didn't think this week could get any better, but you just made me happier than ever. Thank you so much, Joseph. Thank you for everything."

They kissed and hugged as the sun disappeared beyond the horizon. With their agreement, they felt like they had closed a chapter of hardship in their lives and flipped the page to a brighter future. Knowing the effectiveness of the capsules, they were ready to improve themselves until they reached their happy ending—a fairy tale ending.

Cindy knew the journey was going to be difficult, but she was determined to find happiness by any means necessary. She kissed Joseph again, then leaned away from him. Her smile spread from ear to ear. She had always loved Joseph, but now she felt like she was falling in love with another man—a *new* man for a *new* woman.

Eyes shiny with tears of joy, she said, "Everything's going to be okay. Our future will be lovely... wealthy... and healthy. I promise."

8
___

THE WEDDING

"You're looking good, girl," Cindy said, studying her reflection in the mirror in the elevator. "There's still some room for improvement, but so far so good. Some of these guys might even like the extra weight. It's actually kinda sexy."

She had shed nearly 75 pounds in 18 days. She was still overweight, but she was beginning to feel comfortable in her skin. She hadn't seen the human blob on any reflective surfaces since she started taking the miracle capsules. In the elevator mirror, she saw a beautiful, innocent, hopeful young woman looking back at her.

Complementing her curves, her black cape dress reached down to her thighs. She wore a pair of matching high heels. Although she disliked her gut, she enjoyed the view of her own legs.

Thick thighs save lives, she thought with a mischievous smirk on her face. *Is that how the saying goes?*

Ding!

The elevator came to a stop.

Cindy exhaled, then turned towards the sliding doors. Her smile broadened and her eyes glittered with excitement as she walked into the banquet hall. She was impressed by the floor's beauty. It screamed wealth.

A greeter, a man in his early twenties, stood at the bottom of a flight of stairs. He held an iPad and stylus in his hands.

He said, "Welcome. May I have your name, please?"

"Hello. I'm Cindy Moore. I'm Charlotte's–"

"Best friend, right?"

"Yeah," Cindy said, giggling. "I guess I am. I mean, *yes*. Yes, I am."

"She told me all about you. We're so glad you could make it. I'll let her know you've arrived. The party and refreshments are right upstairs. And there's another elevator right around the corner. Let me know if I can help you with anything else."

"I'll do that. Thank you."

She walked up the stairs, watching her every step to avoid tripping over herself. On the reflective marble steps, she could see the beautiful chandeliers sparkling above her.

She looked up at the tall ceiling and whispered, "Jesus, how much does it cost to rent a place like this?"

She stalled at the top of the stairs, feeling like she had reached the highest point in the world. In reality, she was on the 25th floor of the High Tower Club—the tallest building in the city. To her left, past a couple of tables, she saw guests mingling at a bar, sipping on cocktails while chatting about the lounge. She heard faint music playing in the dance hall beyond some doors in front of her. And to her right, there was a peaceful seating area facing a wall of floor-to-ceiling windows.

Cindy walked across the lounge, smiling and waving at everyone who looked her way. Aside from sharing a few mutual acquaintances, she didn't move among Charlotte's social circle. She made her way to the seating area and stared out at the city.

"It's beautiful," she said. "A party in the clouds."

The tower was surrounded by shorter skyscrapers. She recognized a cluster of upscale apartment buildings in the distance. She looked at those homes once a month on an apartment listing website, dreaming of one day settling down in a high-rise condo. She couldn't see her short apartment building from there. The impoverished side of town was hidden behind the concrete jungle, nestled in the skyscrapers' shadows like a dirty secret.

Standing on the 25th floor, Cindy felt empowered. She felt like she had finally reached the top of the ladder of success. It wasn't her party, but she felt like her arrival was something to celebrate.

Staring down at the pedestrians on the street below, she whispered, "I'll be here permanently someday and you, all of you, will stay down there. All of you will be beneath me. That's where you belong after everything you've done to me. All of you will–"

"Cin..."

Charlotte's voice—laced with doubt—interrupted Cindy's quiet speech. Cindy put a big smile on her face, then turned around to face her friend.

"Cin... dee," Charlotte said, taking a long pause between syllables.

"Hey, Char," Cindy said.

There was a moment of silence between them. The chatter from the other guests faded, but their mouths kept moving. The women hesitated—but for different reasons.

Charlotte was awed by Cindy's transformation. From behind, she didn't even recognize her. The greeter had to point to her so she could find her. She felt like she was meeting a different version of Cindy— a version of her from the future or an actress hired to play her friend in a biopic or an alien wearing Cindy's skin over its body. She grew uneasy just looking at her.

Meanwhile, Cindy was left speechless by Charlotte's beauty. She took a mental image of her friend's outfit, hoping to one day replicate it for her own wedding. Charlotte wore a tight white sheath wedding dress. Her silky hair was drawn back behind her head and rolled in a beautiful chignon. Her minimal makeup gave her an air of natural beauty.

A twinge of envy sparked in Cindy's mind, causing her smile to waver. Charlotte's appearance brought her down a notch. *I'm not like her,* she thought. *Not yet.*

The noise in the lounge returned.

Cindy said, "You look... *stunning.* Sorry, I guess I should start by congratulating you on your big day. So, congratulations on your wedding. I'm so happy for you."

"Cindy," Charlotte responded, her voice strained by uncertainty.

"Yeah," Cindy laughed. "Yeah, it's me. You've said my name three times already."

"Yeah, um... I–I'm just a little shaken up."

"What? Why?" Cindy asked, playing dumb.

She knew the answer, but she wanted to act humble. *Beautiful people like to act like they're not beautiful,* she told herself.

In a hushed voice, she asked, "Did something happen with Michael?"

Charlotte said, "No, he's fine. We're fine. It's just... Cindy, you look... incredible. I don't even know what else to say. I just saw you a few weeks ago, but I feel like I haven't seen you in months. How much... Sorry, maybe I shouldn't ask."

"You can ask me anything. What's the big deal? Seriously, go for it."

Charlotte knew Cindy was sensitive about her weight. They spoke about her difficulties losing weight, but they never talked about the specifics. '*How much did you gain? How much did you lose?*' Charlotte never asked those questions because she didn't want to trigger a negative response from her friend. But now Cindy was practically begging to be asked about her transformation.

Charlotte put a fake smile on her face and asked, "How much weight did you lose, hon?"

Cindy said, "Not much. Just about... Let me think, um... I guess about 70 pounds. Maybe closer to 75."

Charlotte's face turned to stone. She said, "Seventy... five. Are you sure you don't mean, like... seven*teen* point five?"

"Of course not. That wouldn't even be *that* noticeable. Don't I look like I've lost a lot of weight?"

"Yeah, that's the thing. You look like a totally different person. How... How did you do this?"

Cindy said, "Well, I don't think I can pretend like I did it through exercise and dieting, so I'll just be honest with you." She leaned in closer to her and said, "I've been getting a little help from a miracle capsule."

"Miracle capsule?"

"It's basically a diet pill. And it's been working wonders. I look and feel better than ever. I never believed in miracles until I took that first capsule."

Charlotte was at a loss for words. She remembered advising Cindy to look into pills to suppress her appetite, but she never thought a pill could help her lose so much weight in so little time.

"Excuse me, Charlotte," the greeter said as he approached the women.

Charlotte looked at the greeter and said, "Yes?"

"Michael's asking for you on the dance floor. He's a little buzzed."

"I'll be right there."

"I'll let him know."

Charlotte looked back at Cindy, grabbed her hands, and in a gentle tone, she said, "Let's talk about this later. I'd really love to take a look at these 'capsules' you've been taking. Maybe they can help me out, too."

Beautiful people like to act like they're not beautiful, Cindy repeated in her head. *Yup, I knew it.*

She said, "Sure. Let's talk later."

Charlotte said, "Great. I'll go check on Michael. You should come dance. Let loose, y'know? I'm sure Joseph won't mind." As she walked away, she said, "I'll find you later, Cin."

"Sounds good. Sounds good..."

Stimulated by a person's imagination, envy came from feelings of entitlement, insecurities, and passion. It spoiled moods and warped minds. It made people think irrationally and act improperly.

Cindy was now filled with envy. She stood in front of the floor-to-ceiling windows with her arms crossed and lips curled in disdain. A part of her wanted to be happy for Charlotte. She attended the reception to celebrate her best friend's big day after all. The other part of her—the bigger, louder part—despised Charlotte for her happiness.

"My day will come, Char," Cindy said. "With or *without* you, my day will come."

"Hello there," a man said from behind Cindy. "Did I hear my name over here?"

Cindy glanced back at the voice, befuddled. A young man approached her. His black hair was styled in a combover and his stubble was trimmed. His face was clean and chiseled. She could tell he took care of his body just by looking at his jawline. Like the rest of the male guests, he wore a tuxedo. He exuded a confident, welcoming aura.

"I'm sorry. I was just mumbling to myself, I guess," Cindy said. "I don't think we've met, so I don't even know your name."

The man stopped next to her and stared out the window. He said, "Nice view, huh?"

"Ye–Yeah. Yeah, it's beautiful."

"You're right. We haven't had the chance to meet. But I had to get your attention somehow. My name is David. David Meyers. It's nice to meet you."

He reached out for a handshake. Cindy wiped her moist palm on her dress, then shook his hand.

She said, "Nice to meet you, too. I'm Cindy."

"You're not here alone, are you?"

Cindy furrowed her brow and leaned away from him a little.

David chuckled, then said, "I don't mean to sound like a creeper. It's just hard to imagine a beautiful woman like yourself showing up to a party like this alone. And if you're not alone, I don't want to run into an angry boyfriend or start any problems. It's a wedding reception. It's time to celebrate, to party—*to love.*"

He's trying to pick me up, Cindy thought, her cheeks turning red and warm.

She said, "Well, you don't have to worry about starting any problems. I'm here alone and..." She paused for five seconds, then said, "And I'm single. So, it's fine. There won't be any drama or anything like that. Are you, um..."

"Am I here alone?"

"Yeah. Are you?"

"I am. I'm one of Michael's friends. I'm not from around here, though. I mean, I was born and raised here, but I don't live here anymore. Just back in town for a week for my bud's wedding. Figured I could reconnect with old friends and... 'mingle' with new ones."

"So, you're *that* type of guy."

She sighed in disappointment, looked back at the window, and crossed her arms again. She was interested in meeting handsome men like David, but she didn't want to be a part of his game. She could see he was a player looking for an easy lay.

"I think you have the wrong idea," David said. "I'm not 'that' guy. Not looking for a one-night stand. Not looking for an 'easy' girl. I'm just looking for someone to talk to. I won't lie: I was drawn to you because you're an attractive woman. But that's not the point. I'm just looking to hang out, y'know? It's all right if you don't want to, but if you're interested, I'm not going to pressure you into anything else. Scout's honor."

Cindy stared into David's glowing blue eyes and thought about his explanation. He seemed sincere and deceitful at the same time. He was looking for a woman to pick up and take home, but he didn't mind working for it.

David asked, "What do you say? Wanna spend a little time together?" He raised his hand in an OK gesture with his thumb and index finger just a millimeter apart. He said, "Just a little?"

Cindy laughed and wagged her head, then said, "I don't know. I'm not... This isn't me. I'm not the girl that guys ask to spend time together with. Look around you. I can't compete with most of the other girls. You sure you want to be seen with someone like me?"

"I wouldn't have approached you if I didn't. As cliché as it may sound, you're my type. I like a full-figured woman with a beautiful face and a shy personality. I really do. So, what do you say? You up for some fun?"

"Okay, okay. I guess we can hang out for a while," Cindy said with a coy smile.

"Great. Now let's break the ice. Let's dance."

"Dance?"

"There's no better icebreaker than a dance-off, is there?"

"Wait, I don't know how to–"

David tugged on Cindy's arm and pulled her away from the windows. Cindy held her other hand over her mouth and giggled as she followed him to the doors at the end of the lounge. As soon as David cracked one of the doors open, their ears were hit with loud music—*I Gotta Feeling* by the Black Eyed Peas—and ceaseless chatter. The floor vibrated with the song's bass.

David led her to the dance floor. With his fists up to his chest, he danced to the music, rocking from side to side. He was relaxed, calm and cool. Cindy wasn't much of a dancer. She peeked at the women around her. Everyone seemed to be flowing effortlessly with the music. *I'll copy them,* she thought. *If they laugh, I'll say I was just joking.*

She smiled, took a step to her left, then a quick step to her right while shaking her shoulders. She snapped her fingers two times before noticing no one else was doing it. She took another step to her left, then her round face twisted into an ugly wad of lines. A sharp pain rocketed from her midsection. She felt like she had been stabbed through her belly button.

She stopped moving and looked down at herself. Her stomach rumbled and moaned loudly, audible over the loud music.

David stopped dancing upon noticing her expression of pain. He asked, "You okay? What's wrong?"

Trying to smile through the agony, Cindy stuttered, "I–I'm... fine. I'm... I'm... Shit..."

"You're shit? You don't look so good. Let's get–"

The partygoers erupted with joyous laughter as *Baby Got Back* by Sir Mix-A-Lot started playing.

Cindy lurched past David. She felt the floor tilting under her and the dancers around her jumped in a great wavelike motion. She felt like she was walking on a boat for the first time, struggling to find her sea legs. To stop herself from collapsing, she leaned on the dancing men and women as she made her way through the crowd. Some of them pushed her away for invading their personal space while others didn't notice her. She teetered over to the ladies' room with her hand on her belly.

Cindy slammed the restroom door behind her and secured its deadbolt. She glanced at the sinks and mirrors to her left, then at the five stalls to her right. She dropped to her knees next to the closest stall, then crawled forward until she could see under all of them. She searched for any straggling women or naughty couples. To her relief, the restroom was empty. She leaned against a stall wall to help her slide up to her feet.

Tired and hurt, she whispered, "What's happening to me? Is it... Is it the capsu–"

Mid-sentence, a gurgling sound came out of her mouth and stopped her from talking. Her stomach rumbled again. It rumbled so hard that she could feel the vibrations in her chest and pelvis. She reeled into the last stall to her right and dropped to her knees. She squeezed her eyes shut and vomited into the toilet.

The puke came out hot and quick. It splashed and sizzled in the water, sending its heat back up to her face in plumes of fetid steam. She couldn't stop vomiting, either. It kept coming out, one big mouthful after another. She felt like a powerful man was strangling her, unable to breathe through her aching windpipe. The sound of her puking was louder than the music outside of the restroom.

The noise disgusted her. *She* disgusted herself. She didn't want to see her mess, so she didn't dare to open her eyes.

Her vomiting ended with one final mouthful of puke and a harsh burp. Toilet water and bits of vomit hit her face. She gasped for air and fell on her ass, then leaned back against the wall to her left and tilted her head back. Tears raced out from between her sealed eyelids. She sobbed for a minute while coughing and rubbing her stinging throat.

"N–No, God, no," she whimpered. "Please s–stop this. It hurts. It–It hurts so much. Please stop it. I was doing so good. I was... I was doing so good, damn it! Why does this always happen to me?!"

Cindy's eyes popped open as her stomach rumbled and growled and squeaked and hissed. She wheezed and held her belly. Beads of sweat covered her exposed skin and wet her dress. Her midsection got hotter and hotter. She felt like she was being burned alive from within. Without looking into the toilet, she pulled her underwear down and sat on the seat.

The restroom door rattled.

"No, no, no," she said, trying to hold it in.

She clenched her sphincter and ass in an attempt to stop herself from defecating, but she couldn't stop it. Against her will, she relieved her bowels along with a burst of flatulence. It sounded like a firecracker was going off in the toilet bowl. She slapped the walls to her left and right and screamed at the top of her lungs. Thick veins stuck out from her neck and forehead and her eyeballs bulged from their sockets.

She felt like she was giving birth to a full-grown man—like all of her organs, big and small, were pouring out through her anus.

"Stop!" she yelled. "Please, *stop!*"

She shut her eyes and slapped her hands over her ears. She didn't want to see the bathroom or hear the excrement plopping in the vomit-filled toilet or think about the guests waiting outside. By retreating into her mind, she sought total silence and darkness—and it worked.

The world around her darkened. The stall walls drifted away from her, taking the stench of puke and feces with them. The noise below her became muffled, then vanished. For a short period of time, she was plucked out of the embarrassing situation and dropped into the abyss.

She had forgotten the benefits of loneliness—the peace, the silence, the self-reflection, the ability to take a shit without being judged. She could finally breathe.

As her involuntary defecation stopped, Cindy opened her eyes and breathed a sigh of relief. The burning sensation in her abdomen fizzled out. Her nausea and dizziness subsided. She wrapped a wad of toilet paper around her shaky fingers and wiped her sore ass, then let the paper fall into the bowl. She wiped four more times, then used the rest of the toilet paper to wipe off the water that had splashed up to the back of her legs and ass.

She struggled to her feet, then froze as she grabbed the toilet's lever. She caught a glimpse of the toilet bowl from the corner of her eye. It was painted red —*dark red*—by the vomit and feces. The chunky mound of feces and puke stuck out of the crimson water like an iceberg. It was a bloody mess, but she couldn't tell if the blood had come out of her ass or mouth—or both. She put her hand over her mouth and nose as she caught a whiff of the stench rising from the bowl. It quickly filled the restroom.

Cindy said, "This can't be because of the capsules. No, no, that's... that's impossible. They worked. I was... feeling good. It... It must have been the food. Yeah, it was the fuckin' *food*. I was eating too much. Nothing's wrong with me. I'm fine. I–I'm going to be okay."

The restroom door rattled again.

Cindy instinctively pushed the toilet's lever down. The bloody water and chunks swirled for five seconds, then a loud *thud* came out of the toilet. It was followed by a gurgling sound.

"Don't do this to me now," Cindy whispered as she pushed down on the lever again. "Not now. Not today."

There was another loud *thud*, then the gurgling noise was joined by hissing and bubbling sounds. The tank shook, then the water started to rise.

"No!" she yelled as she pushed down on the lever repeatedly.

Despite her efforts, the disgusting mixture of blood, crap, and vomit kept rising. Upon reaching the top, the bloody water spilled out from between the toilet seat and the bowl's rim. The liquid streamed down the sides of the toilet, then flowed across the tile floor and out of the stall. Meanwhile, the sludge of shit and feces slid over the toilet seat.

Shaking her head erratically, Cindy stammered, "It-It-It wasn't me. Th–This wasn't me."

She ran out of the stall, feet zigzagging as she slid on the bloody liquid on the floor. She went to a sink and washed her hands. In the mirror, she spotted a piece of shit clinging to her cheek, like a wad of wet toilet paper stuck on the ceiling of a boys' restroom. Thin strings of red puke hung from her lips, too. She shuddered and retched as she washed it off.

After washing herself off, she stared at her reflection and said, "You have to get out of here, Cin. Don't talk to anyone, don't look at anyone. Just. Get. *Out*."

She inhaled deeply, then went over to the door. It rattled every few seconds. Someone was pushing on it from the other side. She heard some muffled voices and music beyond the door, too. She unlocked it and pulled it open.

"God, what were you doing in there?" a young woman asked. "I've been waiting to pee for, like, ten minutes."

"That door's not supposed to be locked," another woman said.

More women were lined up on the wall next to the door. Most of the guests kept dancing on the dance floor, although a few were also looking over at the bathroom door.

Cindy smiled and waved as she walked away in a hurry. *I Ran* by A Flock of Seagulls played on the dance floor. She hustled through the guests in the lounge, then rushed down the stairs.

"Cindy!"

Cindy stopped halfway down the stairs upon hearing her name. She looked behind her and found Charlotte standing at the top of the stairs.

"Where are you going?" she asked. "What happened?"

"Charlotte," Cindy said. "I'm sorry, but I, um... I have to go."

"What are you talking about? You just got here. And you looked like you were having a great time. I saw you dancing with that guy. Did he say something to you? Is everything okay?"

"It's fine. He was fine. Everything's fine. I just... I *really* have to go."

As Charlotte took her first step down, Cindy hurried down the rest of the stairs and called the elevator.

"Are you seriously running from me right now?" Charlotte asked, stunned.

"I'm sorry, but I have to go. There's something I have to do. Congratulations on your wedding, sweetie. Enjoy the rest of your day."

As she reached the bottom of the stairs, Charlotte asked, "Is this about the pills?"

Ding!

The elevator arrived and the doors slid open. Cindy slipped into the empty elevator, pressed the button labeled '1,' then mashed the DOOR CLOSE button repeatedly.

She said, "We'll talk later, Char. I promise. And I'm so sorry."

"Sorry for what?"

Cindy frowned and shrugged at her. The doors slid closed. She leaned against the wall, panting and whining.

9

PROGRESS

LIKE A PRETENTIOUS PERVERT, CINDY GAWKED AT HER reflection in the rearview mirror. She could no longer recognize herself—and that fact titillated her. She stroked her strong cheekbones and defined jawline. Her fingers stopped over her glossy pink lips. Then she snickered as she slid her palm under her chin and pushed up on her jaw.

"Only one chin. A little loose, but better than two," she said. "Less than a month and I already look like *this*. Miracles really can happen."

She got out of her car with a peppy bounce and slammed the door behind her. She checked her outfit on the door's reflection, posing next to her car like a model at an auto show. She wore a loose blank tank top over a matching sports bra and skintight leggings. Brimming with confidence, she strutted into the gym.

She even winked and smirked at the male employee behind the front desk.

"Oops," she said as she bumped into someone near the stationary bikes. "I'm so..."

Her voice trailed off, but her lips kept moving. She was surprised to see Deki, sweaty and panting, standing next to her. Simultaneously shy and flirty, she put one hand on her hip and the other over her cheek.

"Hey," she said. "It's been a while, hasn't it?"

Deki was dumbstruck. Face twitching with anxiety and horror, his eyes shrank into a squint, then grew, then shrank again. Trying to see the bigger picture, he took two steps back and continued looking her up and down. He sold dreams for a living, but at that very moment, he felt like his life had turned into a nightmare.

"Cin–Cindy?" he stuttered. "Cindy Moore?"

Swinging her hips seductively, Cindy spun around slowly. After finishing the rotation, she lowered her arms with her palms facing Deki and grinned, like a magician saying '*Ta-da!*' after a magic trick.

"Yup," she said. "It's me. It's the *real* me, Deki. What do you think? Not to sound cocky, but I'm looking pretty good, aren't I?"

"You, um... You look fantastic," Deki replied, a trace of reluctance in his voice. He gave a fake laugh, then said, "Those capsules worked wonders on you just like I said. I don't think you have to lose any more weight.

This look right here... This is working for you. This *is* you."

"Thank you. I couldn't have done it without you. But I can't stop now. I can do better than this. I know it."

As if he were a real doctor, Deki examined her again. Aside from the fading scars on her arm and hand, he didn't detect any troubling side effects.

He said, "I'm sorry for asking this. It's not that you're forgettable. I'm just forgetful. Remind me... when exactly did I sell you those capsules?"

Cindy hummed and looked up at the ceiling. She already knew the answer to the question—she was meticulously keeping track of her weight loss progress after all—but she wanted to keep Deki on his toes so she could surprise him. She loved watching people's jaws drop when she spoke about her experience with the miracle capsules. Her eyes dropped to Deki's.

She said, "Less than four weeks ago. Probably 25 days. Something like that. Pretty impressive, huh?"

"*Twenty-five days?*" Deki repeated. He took another step back and glanced around the gym, as if he were looking for a prank show's hidden camera crew. He said, "You're lying. Tell me you're lying. Tell me this is part of a–a–a joke."

"What? Why would I lie about that?"

"Cindy, how much have you lost since you started taking the capsules? Hmm? No offense, but you were *huge* the last time I saw you."

Cindy cocked her head back, offended. She said, "Wow. You weren't that honest when you were selling me your 'medicine.' Well, I'm not *huge* anymore, am I?"

"How much have you lost, Cindy?"

"A little over a hundred pounds now. Jeez, what's up with your attitude? I thought you'd–"

"A hundred pounds?! You have..."

His voice trailed off into an indistinct mumble when he realized he was shouting. The employee behind the front desk and a couple patrons on the stationary bikes looked their way.

"You have to be kidding me," he said angrily. "That's too much weight in too little time. You're losing weight faster than anyone I've ever 'treated' before. How much are you eating? You *are* eating as much as possible, right? You've been following my instructions, haven't you?"

Cindy breathed out a mix of disappointment and annoyance. She shook her head as she stared down at her new running shoes. She had been hoping she would impress him with her results. She wanted him to praise her, to hug her, to ask her out on a date. Instead, he reminded her of Joseph and Charlotte. She mistook his concern for jealousy.

They just don't want to see me succeed, she thought.

She didn't want to admit the truth to him, though. After her frightening experience in the High Tower Club's restroom, she started ignoring Deki's instructions and began limiting her meals. She stopped eating and drinking anything red entirely. The color reminded her of the feces and vomit in the toilet. She tried to convince herself that food dye had changed the color of her waste.

"I appreciate your concern, but you don't have to worry about me," she said. "As you can see, I'm doing fine without you. I know how to take care of myself. If this is about the money, I know I still owe you a little. But like I told you in my email, I'll send the rest as soon as my, um, 'friend' pays me. You don't have to get all worked up about it."

Deki said, "I'm not worried about the money. I'm just... I need to make sure that you're okay. If you get sick, you'll end up bringing the wrong type of attention to *my* door. I don't want that. Look, you're losing weight much faster than usual and that tells me that you're not eating as much as you should be eating. Am I right?"

"You're wrong. I'm just watching what I eat. I don't want to eat too much and gain all of that weight back. I'm trying to balance it out. Seriously, stop worrying about it. I know what I'm doing."

"You don't," Deki said sternly. He leaned in closer to her and whispered, "Listen and listen closely, you have to eat as much as possible throughout the day or whenever you're awake, especially if you're still taking the capsules. If you don't keep up with them, the 'medicine' will *consume* you. It will literally eat you from the inside. Once you're out of fat and muscle and even skin, it'll start eating away at your organs and even your bones. That includes your brain. It'll change you physically and mentally. You understand me?"

Cindy clenched her jaw and nodded, like a child being scolded by a teacher.

Deki asked, "Have you had any internal bleeding? Have you vomited any blood? Or had any blood in your stool? You know, your crap? Do you ever taste blood in your mouth?"

The answer was the same for each question: *Yes.* But Cindy stopped herself from blurting it out. She was afraid she would end up in a hospital and the capsules would be taken from her if she told the truth. She was already regretting giving a few to Joseph. She wasn't willing to let go of her last batch. She was too close to the finish line to give up.

"I'm fine," she said.

Deki said, "You have to follow the directions I gave you. I can write 'em down again if you–"

"*I'm fine,*" Cindy repeated, raising her voice.

They gazed into each other's eyes, listening to the wheezing around them and the pop music from the gym's sound system.

Deki said, "Good or bad, there are consequences for all of our actions. There's a price for everything. Nothing in this world is free. If you continue to ignore me, you might end up paying much more than $1,000. Be careful, Cindy."

He patted her shoulder, then walked away. His touch was gentle and the look in his eyes was one of sincere sympathy. He sought riches, but he wasn't evil. He was a drug dealer with a conscience.

Cindy watched him walk out. She was unnerved by his warning, but she refused to give up the capsules. She kept repeating the same sentence in her head: *Everything's going to be okay. Everything's going to be okay. Everything's going to be okay.*

Cindy jogged on a treadmill. She heard her *thumping* footsteps, but the machine didn't groan or rattle like it did before her dramatic weight loss. Her footsteps merged with the noise from the other runners. For the first time since she signed up for the gym, she didn't feel like she was being judged. She felt like a regular person doing some regular exercise.

She smiled at her reflection in the mirror in front of her. The miracle capsules had killed off the human blob. She felt like she was finally seeing her true self.

Between breaths, Cindy whispered, "Almost done... Almost perfect... Just another week... Maybe two... I can do this. I can—"

She grimaced and staggered as a jolt of pain rocked her right leg. She grabbed onto the handrail and tapped a button on the control panel to reduce the treadmill's speed. As she slowed to a stroll, she felt a burning sensation on her thigh, as if someone were pressing a hot curling iron against her leg. Her stroll turned into a limp.

She slowed the treadmill down to a pace of 0.5 miles per hour. The red button at the center of the control panel attracted her eyes. It read: *EMERGENCY*. She was too embarrassed to stop and too proud to ask for help, though. A ball of blistering pain, growing hotter by the second, bobbled back and forth between her knee and hip.

"Fuck," she moaned as she leaned over the control panel.

Unable to continue walking, Cindy pressed the treadmill's PAUSE button. It gave her sixty seconds to decide to carry on or stop. If she didn't decide, the exercise would stop automatically at the end of the countdown. She paid it no mind. She straightened her leg, as if stretching would help ease the pain. *It's just a cramp,* she thought, trying to stop herself from panicking. *Or maybe I just pulled a muscle.*

She glanced over at one of the treadmills to her right. A thirtysomething guy in a sleeveless t-shirt and denim shorts kept peeking over at her. He was curious about her situation, but he looked like he didn't want to get involved. He was dressed like he didn't want to be in the gym in the first place.

Cindy smiled and waved at him. She was about to tell him that she was fine when her treadmill *beeped*. Her sixty-second break was up and the exercise automatically ended. She grabbed her water bottle and hobbled away from the treadmills. She stopped in the gym's designated stretching area. She was supposed to take off her shoes before stepping onto the mats, but she couldn't crouch or bend over.

On her good foot, she hopped across the mats. She grabbed onto the Pilates barre attached to the mirrors and stretched. She moved her hurt leg in every direction, twisting it this way and that way, but her efforts were fruitless.

"Goddammit," she hissed through her gritted teeth.

She limped into the woman's locker room next to the stretching area. Two women stood in front of the sinks to her left, snapping selfies for their social media accounts. Some women changed clothes at the lockers to the right. At the end of the room, a doorway led to a restroom. And a doorway in the restroom opened up to the shower room, which was connected to a pool and sauna.

Cindy made her way into a stall in the restroom. She sat on the toilet and pulled her leggings down to her knees.

"Oh my God," she said weakly.

Her quadriceps were bruised like a banana, black and brown. Surrounded by small patches of grayish skin, the dark bruises blotched most of her thigh.

"What happened to me?" Cindy whispered as she gaped at her leg. "I–I didn't hit myself... did I? No, n–no, I only... I bumped into Deki, but that wasn't enough to do something like this. No, it's impossible. It wasn't like this when I woke up, was it? I... I... would have noticed it. It must..."

She stopped talking to herself upon noticing the silence in the restroom. The women in the locker room had stopped talking. She assumed they were eavesdropping. People were naturally curious.

"Bitches," Cindy muttered. "Mind your own damn business."

She cringed as she poked her injured thigh. The gentle touch ignited an aching pain in her leg. Her skin was grainy like asphalt. Baffled by the unusual texture, she gently scratched the bruise, as if she were peeling a scab. She scraped black flakes of skin off her thigh, revealing a spot of dark gray, pudding-like tissue.

Eyes big and wild, she poked the abnormal flesh. The tip of her finger sank *into* her thigh. Like pus from a popped pimple, a jet of blood flew out and hit the stall wall. She shrieked in pain. It only took about two seconds for her fear of embarrassment to take control of her body. She slapped her other hand over her mouth, ground her teeth, and held her breath while rocking from side to side on the toilet.

Her fingertip was stuck in her thigh. She felt her wet and mushy muscle. The slightest movement of her trapped finger caused waves of agony to ripple through her body. And the pain made her stomach knot up, leaving her woozy and nauseated. A ring of blood circled her finger. Cold sweat and warm tears dribbled across her scrunched, ashy face.

"Hello?" a woman called out from the restroom's entrance. "Everything okay in here?"

Cindy breathed out through her nose, launching webs of snot over her hand. She snorted some of it back into her nostrils along with some fresh air, then took her hand off her mouth.

"Ye–Yes," she whimpered, trying to stay as still as possible.

The restroom was silent for ten seconds.

The other woman said, "I work here. If you need any assistance, you can tell me."

"I–I'm fine, really," Cindy replied. The employee didn't say a word or take a step. Cindy laughed to try to reduce her suspicion, then said, "I'm sorry, I just saw a spider in the toilet and I freaked out a little."

The woman said, "Okay. Well, if you need anything, I'll be in the locker room."

Boring the pain, Cindy put her hand over her mouth and gritted her teeth. *Leave, bitch, leave!* She wanted to reply, but she bottled her anger by holding her breath. After another ten seconds of silence, the employee walked away.

Cindy waited for a minute, then shoved the collar of her shirt into her mouth. After three deep breaths, she yanked her finger out of her leg. Drops of blood splashed on the door and floor. She grunted and squeezed her eyes shut. Within seconds, her face went from pale to red with thick veins slithering across her brow.

Close to losing consciousness, she swayed on the toilet seat. Her head bobbed and shook violently. A tingly feeling spread across her mutated thigh. The pain started to subside after three minutes, and it took her another two minutes to calm herself.

"Fu–Fuck," she whined.

She looked down at the floor upon hearing a *plopping* sound. Blood was dripping onto the tiles under her from her leg. She frowned at her finger. It was covered in the darkest blood she had ever seen. If it weren't for the light in the room, she would have mistaken it for black ink.

She wiped the sweat, tears, and mucus off her face with her shirt, then grabbed a toilet paper roll from the stall wall. Creating a makeshift bandage, she wrapped the toilet paper around her mutilated thigh until only the paperboard core was left. The dark blood seeped through the sheets, but it was enough to slow and hide the bleeding.

As she carefully lifted her leggings, she said, "I... have... to eat."

Cindy shambled out of the restroom, leaving her bloody mess behind. In the locker room, she found the female employee wiping a bench down with a towel.

The woman looked at her and asked, "That spider still in there?"

"I flushed it," Cindy said.

"Oh. Did you need any..."

Cindy limped away before the employee could finish speaking. She saw the two young women at the sinks near the entrance.

As she moved past them, one of the women said, "Aren't you going to wash your hands?"

"Fuck off, you stupid bitch," Cindy responded as she hobbled to the exit.

"Excuse *me?*"

"What's your problem, bitch?" her friend said.

Cindy didn't give them another second of her time. She limped out of the gym and went straight to her car. She raced home, trying to escape another humiliating nightmare.

10

EAT OR BE EATEN

THE CELL PHONE BUZZED ACROSS THE NIGHTSTAND WHILE playing *Bitch Better Have My Money* by Rihanna. Only the light from the screen pierced the darkness in the bedroom.

Face planted in her pillow, Cindy reached blindly for the phone. She pushed the lamp off the nightstand. A tissue box followed it to the floor. The phone slid around like a bar of soap on a wet shower floor. Groaning in frustration, she lifted her head from the pillow and snatched it off the nightstand. She was annoyed to see Charlotte's picture and name on the screen. In her notification area, there were seven missed calls—all from Charlotte and all at perfect thirty-minute intervals.

Cindy muted her phone before returning it to the nightstand. The lamp and tissue box stayed on the floor. She rolled onto her back and stared absently at the dusty ceiling. She was exhausted and apathetic, unable to interact normally with the world. The capsules had sent her on the ride of her life, but now that roller coaster was plummeting to the deepest depths of her misery. She wanted to sleep the pain away, but she knew it wasn't an option.

Depression was chronic—there in the morning, there at bedtime, there in dreams and nightmares.

She sat on the edge of her bed and looked down at her legs. Both of her thighs were bruised now. The hole on her right leg was bandaged with a gauze roll. Her weight loss continued at an alarming rate. Due to her lethargy, she didn't have the energy to fight the side effects of the capsules. She couldn't go to the super-market to stock up on food because she was too weak to carry the groceries. And after spending so much money on the capsules, she couldn't afford to order takeout for every meal of the day, either.

Eyes glossy with tears, Cindy glanced at her phone and said, "Maybe I should just give up. Maybe... Maybe I should call Charlotte back. Or Joseph. Or... Or an ambulance." She put her hands over her face and whimpered, "What did I do to myself? God, why did I do this? I'm going to end up dead. He was right. They were all right. I messed–"

She belched. It was so sudden that it jolted her like a jump scare in a horror movie. She drew a deep breath and, mid-inhale, belched again.

"God," she groaned with her hand over her mouth.

She stumbled into her bathroom. She moaned in agony as she fell to her knees in front of the sink. Blood oozed out of the hole on her thigh, staining the bandage with a big red dot. Pushing through the pain, she shimmied over to the toilet, pushed the seat up, then belched again before barfing. She closed her eyes tight as the thick vomit plunged into the water and splattered on the bowl. She panted for a few moments, then puked again.

And just a few seconds after that, she puked a third time.

She was left breathless, throat and tongue stinging. As her nausea subsided, she leaned over the seat and flushed the toilet. She was disgusted by the bloody chunks of vomit but relieved to see the water swirl down the drain without a hitch. She rested her cheek on the seat and stared into the bowl as it refilled. Little red flakes of puke floated in the water. Beads of blood slid down the sides of the bowl, too.

Her tears plopping in the water, Cindy murmured, "Am I dying?"

She approached the full-body mirror standing next to the dresser in the living room. She had purchased it about a week after taking her first dose of Deki's miracle medicine so she could see the results. As her vision adjusted to the darkness, she began to make herself out in the mirror. She lifted her loose black t-shirt and studied her body.

Despite achieving her dreams and losing over 130

pounds, she was disgusted with herself. The human blob that had followed her on every reflective surface was replaced by a distorted, unshapely figure.

Her breasts had shriveled up, deep wrinkles stretching away from her inverted nipples. A large pouch of loose skin hung over her black panties like a fanny pack. Loose, wrinkled skin drooped from her limbs, too. Her arms and legs were still thick while the fat across her abdomen burned at an accelerated rate. At 150 pounds, her ribs were visible, sticking out like a starved dog.

As she stared down at her bulging bones, Cindy whispered, "I couldn't see them last night. What's happening to my body?" She brought her eyes back to the mirror. She said, "Parts of me are still fat and others are... are *skinny*. And my skin is... It looks like it's stretching. What the hell is going on? Did the... Did the fat just *move*? Is that even possible?"

She couldn't think of a reasonable explanation for her bizarre weight loss. She looked down at her rib cage again. Her curiosity got the best of her. She touched one of her ribs, then she ran her finger across it gently, like a musician playing a glass harp. It was tender, but it didn't hurt as much as her legs. She made an OK sign with her hand, then flicked the rib with her index finger.

"*Ow!*" she screeched.

She staggered back with both of her hands cupped over the left side of her rib cage. She fell back on her sofa. A throbbing pain emanated from her rib—an awful pain that worsened with each panicked breath. She felt like she had cracked her own rib. *It's impossible,* she told herself. *Impossible. Totally impossible! Completely impossible!* She bit her lip and slowed her breathing.

The pain relented after three minutes.

Cindy leaned over and turned on the lamp. Too tired to pick it up, she left it on the floor next to the tissue box. She got to her feet and hobbled over to the mirror.

"What have I done to myself?" she said.

Dark, circular bruises were scattered across most of her body in a polka dot pattern. Pink rashes with stripes of petechiae broke out around the bruises. The bruises on her legs were the largest and darkest. Her stomach, although sagging, remained white. The texture of the skin around her belly button caught her attention. It had the texture of soured milk, chunky and slimy.

Is it melting fat or rotting skin? she thought.

She caressed the skin around her belly button with her fingertip, as if trying to tickle herself. She didn't feel anything. Her finger stopped over her belly button. Echoes of pain from her rib reminded her of her earlier experiment. Yet, like a person with an excoriation disorder, she couldn't stop herself from picking at her skin.

She eased her pudgy finger into her cavernous

belly button. It slid in without any resistance—and it kept going and going. Her eyes expanded with fear and disgust. Over an *inch* of her finger was *in* her navel. She felt like she had put her finger into a bowl of oatmeal, wet and mushy. It didn't hurt, though. She wiggled her finger around.

Cindy gasped as she pulled her finger out. It was coated in dark blood. It streamed down to her palm. Then she heard the loud splashing below her. Her eyes grew even larger as she stared down at her body. Blood poured out of her belly button like water from a downspout.

"Shit! Shit! Shit!" she shouted.

Hands over her stomach, she rushed into the bathroom. She wrapped half a roll of toilet paper around her hand, then folded it over two times. It looked like a flimsy joint. She stuffed it into her belly button to clog the leak. Her blood rapidly soaked through the paper plug, but it stopped trickling out.

"No, no, no," Cindy said, words racing out of her mouth. "I–I have to do something."

Trembling all over, Cindy returned to her bed. She grabbed her cell phone and dialed 911. Her thumb hovered over the green DIAL prompt. She wanted to admit defeat and call for help, but then she heard something at the back of her head. It sounded like ocean waves in the distance at first. Seconds later, it turned into a faint hum before growing into an indistinct murmur.

Then she recognized it.

The little voice had returned.

Don't, it hissed. *They're all going to laugh at you. They'll take your picture and share it with the world. Do you want the world to see you like this, you nasty bitch?*

Cindy stared at the mass of bloodied, wrinkled loose skin on her lap. She began to tear up while swaying back and forth. She felt lightheaded and her body stiffened up. Her insecurities struck fear into her heart—irrational but *raw* fear. Upon realizing she was holding her breath, she exhaled shakily.

"I can't," she said as she wiped her face with the back of her hand. "Not them. No–Not anyone who knows me."

She scrolled through her contact list. She stopped on Deki's name. She figured he was the only person who could help her and the only person who wouldn't judge her. She called him and held the phone up to her ear.

"Please pick up," she whispered as she listened to the shrill ringback tone. "Please help me. Please–"

"Hello?" Deki answered.

"Deki! Oh, thank God!"

"Yeah," Deki replied with uncertainty. "Uh... Who's this?"

"Cindy. It's Cindy from the gym. Thank you so

much for answering. You don't know how much that means to me."

"Cindy, um... I'm sorry, but what is this about? What's going on?"

"Right, right. I'm sorry to bother you. I'm just... I'm going through something over here. You see, I think... No, I *know* I'm sick. I'm very, *very* sick, Deki, and I think it's because of the capsules."

"You're sick?"

"*Very.*"

The call fell silent for ten uncomfortable seconds.

"Okay," Deki said. "Let's get this straightened out. What exactly are you feeling? What are your symptoms? And most importantly, how long have you been feeling sick? And be as specific as possible, Cindy."

Cindy bit her bottom lip and shook her head. She tracked the beginning of her sickness back to Charlotte's wedding reception. Since then, she had been frequently vomiting and defecating blood. Her body had only recently begun to soften and morph.

She sighed, then said, "I lied to you, Deki. I was sick when you saw me at the gym last week and I was sick the week before that. I've been puking and... and *shitting* out blood. I was just too embarrassed to admit it. I know it's stupid and I screwed up. I know that already. I'm so sorry for not telling you. But you have to help me. I don't... I..." She sobbed and dry-heaved for a few seconds, then said, "I don't want to die. Please, Deki, help me."

Deki fell silent again. Only his heavy breathing came through the phone's speaker. The confession rattled him.

"I understand," he said in a tight voice. He grunted, then said, "So, you're most likely bleeding internally. I think it might still be fixable, but..."

"But *what?*"

"You have to be completely honest with me, Cindy. Have there been any other symptoms? Are you feeling lightheaded? Bleeding from anywhere else? Is your skin... Shit, how do I say this? Um... Just tell me if your skin has been changing, okay? And tell me the truth. I can't help you unless you're 100 percent honest with me."

"I'm a mess," Cindy explained. "I'm falling apart. I have bruises and rashes everywhere. My skin is loose. It's like... like it's melting or something. My bones hurt when I tap 'em. I flicked my rib and I felt like I broke it. Then I... I poked a *hole* into my stomach! I wasn't even trying to do that! I just poked it and blood started coming out! That's not right, *right?* I'm going... God, I'm going to die, aren't I? It–It's over, isn't it?"

Cindy held her clenched fist over her mouth and fidgeted on the bed as she waited for Deki to respond. The fake doctor cycled through the knowledge in his cluttered mind, searching for a solution to Cindy's problem. In his years of selling the miracle capsules, he had never had a customer suffer from so many negative side effects.

He said, "I know this is going to sound crazy, Cindy, but it sounds like you're being eaten from the inside."

"Wha–What?"

"I told you this could happen."

"But that... that can't be true. Wha–What's in my body? What did I put in my body, Deki?"

"Damn it, you really should have called me sooner."

"I'm sorry," Cindy cried.

Deki said, "Don't waste your energy apologizing to me. If it's really as bad as you say, I have to assume you haven't been eating like I told you to. Hell, I'm guessing you haven't been eating much at all. So, listen carefully 'cause this might be the last time I can tell you this. Here's what you're going to do: *Eat.* You hear me? I need you to eat as much as possible and I need you to pray that the food reverses the side effects."

"Eat? Like, a–anything? Is that it?"

"It's exactly what I told you before, isn't it?"

"I thought you were joking. I didn't think eating would actually work for my diet or protect me. It just didn't make sense to me. Food was my problem, not my answer."

"Well, it's your only solution now. Eat, Cindy. If you don't, the 'medicine' in your body will start to consume your skin, your muscles, your organs, your bones... *everything.* You're running out of time. *Eat* or be *eaten.* Good luck."

Cindy said, "Wait, Deki. What do I eat? How do I

know when it's been reversed? Deki?" She looked at the phone's screen. Deki had ended the call. She said, "Eat or be eaten..."

She barreled into the kitchen and opened the refrigerator. A look of dismay dawned on her face. Due to her strict diet and lack of grocery shopping, it was almost empty. She took out a bundle of carrots and a carton of orange juice. She opened the carton while gnawing on the carrots, each bite *crunchier* than the last. She even ate the stems and leaves, too. Then, mouth full of chewed carrots, she chugged the juice. It cascaded down her chin, neck, and chest.

She wasn't sure if the beverage would help offset the medicine's negative side effects, but she hoped the calories or the juice's pulp would help her stay alive. After finishing the carton, she chomped through her last carrot—from the tip to the stem in ten seconds. Pieces of carrot stuck between her teeth and orange juice dripping from her lower lip, she turned and looked into the refrigerator with frenzied eyes. The empty shelves taunted her.

As she glanced at the refrigerator door, she said, "*Butter.*"

She took it out and unwrapped its aluminum foil, then took a big bite of the cold butter, as if she were peeling and eating a banana. She gagged due to its pungent taste, but she refused to slow down. She leaned over the counter and grabbed a jar of peanut butter from a cupboard above her. She shoved the butter into the jar, then prodded it and stirred it with a large spoon until it was all one creamy beige-colored substance.

She shoved a spoonful of it into her mouth. It dried up her tongue and throat instantly. While smacking her tongue around like a dog eating peanut butter, she filled a glass of water at the sink. She guzzled it down to help her swallow. She felt like she wasn't moving fast enough, though. So, she threw the spoon aside and dipped her fingers into the jar. She grabbed a handful of the paste and forced it into her mouth. She needed another glass of water to get it down.

"Can't... stop," she said, the peanut butter and butter mix plastered on her teeth.

She put her hand into the jar and clawed for another handful of the spread. Then she yelped as *popping* and *crunching* sounds came out of the jar. Two seconds later, as a searing pain surged up her right arm, her yelp turned into a full-on shriek. Hand stuck in the jar, she wobbled back, crashed into the kitchen table, then stumbled to her right. Knees on the verge of buckling, she caught herself on a counter next to the refrigerator.

"Ouch, ouch," she whined.

She stayed there for a minute, sobbing and wheezing and shaking. Then, with her free hand, she slowly twisted the jar until she freed her other hand. She gasped. Her middle finger was broken, bent to the side at the center.

Her index finger was severed at the distal interphalangeal joint—*the fingertip*. Blood came out of the wound in short squirts. Meanwhile, the detached fingertip was stuck in the homemade spread. Now, her blood made it look like some strawberry jam was mixed into it.

The insufferable pain from the amputation left Cindy weak and the sight of her blood made her queasy. She hobbled towards the counter in front of her. She wrapped a thick paper towel around her mutilated finger to stop the bleeding. The pain stole her appetite, too—but not her will to live. She grabbed her cell phone and sat on her sofa. Although she wished to keep her deformities to herself, she knew she couldn't survive without a helping hand.

Deki was out of the question. She thought about phoning a neighbor, but she didn't know them very well. An ambulance was her best bet, but the little voice in her head wouldn't allow her to call 911. Even with death knocking at her door, she refused to be seen in public. In her contact list, she pressed Charlotte's name. She hesitated with her finger over the CALL prompt. *She'll probably call an ambulance as soon as she sees me,* she thought.

She looked at her reflection in the mirror across from her. She was pale and sweaty, shuddering ceaselessly. The pain from her finger continued pulsing through her arm in sync with her quick heartbeat. Admitting defeat, she tapped the CALL prompt and held the phone up to her ear. The call connected after two rings.

"Cindy," Charlotte said, sounding giddy with relief. "Hey, hon, I've been trying to get ahold of you for a while now."

"Hey, Char," Cindy said. She was smiling through her tears, but she didn't know why. Speaking slowly to try to stop her voice from breaking, she said, "I'm sorry to call you like this, but I, um... Well, I need your help."

"What's the matter?"

"I can't explain it over the phone."

"Is this about the 'thing' that happened at my wedding reception? I've been wanting to talk to you about that. I'm not angry or anything–"

"Charlotte, it's too hard to explain like this. You just need to know that it's an emergency. It's a..."

Cindy choked up. She didn't want to finish her sentence because she was afraid of the truth. She didn't want to hear it come out of her own mouth.

"What is it?" Charlotte asked.

"It's a... a life-or-death situation."

"*What?* Do you need me to call the cops? Or an ambu–"

"I only need you to listen to me," Cindy interrupted. "Please, Charlotte, just listen to me."

"O–Okay, sure. I'm listening, Cin. What's going on? What do you need me to do?"

Cindy looked at her reflection in the mirror again. Her face was smeared with peanut butter, orange juice glistened on her neck, and bits of carrots clung to her lips. The hole in her stomach was clogged with toilet paper and a bloody paper towel was wrapped around her hand. She was falling apart.

She said, "I need you to bring me two double Westerns, large fries, large onion rings, chicken tenders, and a strawberry milkshake from Carl's. There's one close to my place." Charlotte didn't respond. Cindy said, "Actually, make it three double Western burgers. Three, okay?"

Charlotte's silence continued for another five seconds, then she burst into a giggle. She asked, "What the hell are you talking about? Is this a joke?"

"Bring me the food as soon as possible. I mean, drop whatever you're doing and *hurry*. I don't have much time left."

"Hold up a second, Cin. Are you being serious right now? What is this about?"

"I told you already. It's a life-or-death situation. This is not a joke. Please hurry. *Please*. I love you, Charlotte."

"You're seriously scaring–"

Cindy ended the call and muted her phone. She couldn't bear to hear her best friend's concerns. She didn't know how to explain herself over the phone anyway. She sat quietly and stared at her monstrous reflection while ignoring Charlotte's calls.

"Please hurry," she whispered.

11

FRIENDS THROUGH THICK AND THIN

GLASS SHARDS FROM BROKEN CUPS SPARKLED ON THE kitchen counters. They had fallen from the cupboards above. The jar of peanut butter, licked clean, was on its side next to the shards. An empty carton of orange juice, an empty gallon of milk, and crumpled wrapper of string cheese were scattered on the linoleum floor in front of the refrigerator. Some of the shelves in the fridge were broken. It had been ransacked.

Cindy sat on the floor in front of the refrigerator, back against a dining chair. She held her severed fingertip in her good hand. It was covered in bloody peanut butter. She had considered putting it in ice in hopes of getting it reattached. But she was now completely out of food and her stomach growled with demands for more. Her appetite had returned with full force.

Do it, the little voice in her head said.

"Do what?" Cindy responded aloud, her voice raspy.

Do what you know you have to do.

"But I'm scared."

And hungry. Eat or be eaten.

Cindy slowly raised the fingertip up to her mouth. She whimpered as it touched her trembling lips. She could smell the peanut butter and taste the blood at the back of her mouth.

"Eat or be eaten," she whispered.

She licked the fingertip. The blood strengthened the salty flavor of the sweet, nutty peanut butter. Her taste buds tingled and her tongue quivered. She slurped the rest of the peanut butter, then she nibbled on the finger. She couldn't break the skin with her small bites, so she chomped down on it harder. The fingernail cracked. She spit it out, then bit the finger again.

Fresh blood oozed out of the exposed nail bed. Her incisor teeth sank into the fingertip, directly in front of the bone. She jerked her head back and tore the chunk of flesh off. The rest of the finger slipped out of her hand and fell on the floor. She chewed and swished the skin around in her mouth like a flavorful wad of gum. With each bite, she felt like the piece of skin got larger.

She choked it down with a loud *gulp*, then gasped for air. Although she got it down, she felt like it was still stuck in her throat. She tasted nothing but blood.

And it reinvigorated her.

She picked up the fingertip from the floor. Holding it as if she were eating corn on the cob, she started biting around the finger, peeling the layers of skin off with her teeth. Once it was skinless, she put it in her mouth and sucked the blood from it. She chewed on the bone, too, but she couldn't break it. So, she spit it out.

She instinctively started slurping the blood off her fingers, as if she had just finished eating a plate of fried chicken. She stopped, middle finger in her mouth, as she caught a glimpse of her injured hand.

It was as if she had snapped out of a trance and the truth finally hit her: She had cannibalized herself. Doctors couldn't reattach the fingertip digesting in her stomach. But, although she was revolted by her own actions, she was still hungry. The thought of chopping off another piece of her finger popped into her mind.

"No," she said. "There has to be another way."

She opened the cupboard under the sink. She saw the sink pipes, a bottle of dish soap and another of liquid clog remover, and a bunch of plastic bags. None of it was edible. She squinted at the back of the cupboard. Big, reddish-brown cockroaches skittered around behind the cleaning supplies. She focused on a dead cockroach on its back amongst the intrusion.

Cindy grimaced as she grabbed it. *How much protein does a cockroach contain?* she thought. She didn't have time to do any research. Her body needed more food.

"Don't think about it," she said with tears in the corners of her eyes.

She closed her eyes and put the cockroach in her mouth. She gagged as it rolled towards her uvula. She thrust her head forward to move the cockroach in her mouth, then pushed the insect towards her cheek with her tongue. She bit into it with her molar teeth. It exploded in her mouth with a loud *crunch*. A string of its entrails flew out and hit the back of her throat, causing her to retch.

Tears flew from her face as she shook her head. She kept chewing on the cockroach. It sounded like she was eating toasted bread while her breath was a musty mix of rancid and sweet odors. She swallowed it, then burped. Some of the cockroach's legs and innards were caught between her teeth. She picked the pieces out with her tongue and swallowed them, too.

As she caught her breath, she looked at the cockroaches in the cupboard, then at her hands. She was surprised to find that she preferred cannibalism over entomophagy.

"Maybe just one more fingertip," she said. Someone knocked on her front door. She looked over at the entrance, then down at herself. She said, "They can't see me like this."

She scrambled away from the cupboard and got to her feet near the front door. Through the peephole, she could see Charlotte waiting in the hallway outside. She held a plastic bag with two brown paper bags inside of it and a milkshake in her other hand.

"Cindy!" Charlotte hollered as she kicked the door three times. "It's Charlotte! Open up! Your milkshake's freezing my hand out here!"

Cindy carefully unlocked the door so as not to make any noise, then tiptoed into the apartment and crouched behind the kitchen bar. She didn't want to scare Charlotte off before she could even enter the apartment. She had to ease her into the situation before revealing herself.

"Come in!" Cindy shouted. "The door's unlocked!"

The doorknob jiggled around for a few seconds, then the hinges grated as the door swung open. Charlotte stood in the doorway.

"What's going on?" she asked with her eyebrows raised. "Where are you, Cin? *Cindy?*"

From behind the counter, Cindy said, "Come in and close the door behind you. I'll tell you everything —*show* you everything—but I need to make sure you won't abandon me."

"Oh, *please*, hon. When have I ever abandoned you? Let's stop being melodramatic for a minute, okay? I came here because *you* called *me*. I went out and bought the food you asked for, like your personal Uber Eats driver. And I didn't tell anyone about this. I respected your wishes and your privacy. So, how about you start doing the same? What's going on? What is this?"

"I don't look 'good,' Char. I mean, I don't look like me. Just do me one last favor and then I'll tell you everything. Please, just come in and close the door behind you. I'll beg you if I have to."

A sense of foreboding crawled up Charlotte's throat. She leaned into the apartment and looked around. She couldn't see any of the bloodstains, but she saw the mess in the kitchen clearly. It looked like it had been pillaged.

Charlotte said, "Cindy, is there someone here with you?"

"It's only me, Char, I promise. I wouldn't let anyone else see me like this."

Charlotte entered the apartment and closed the front door with her foot. She walked into the living room, unaware of Cindy's position. She stopped at the foot of the bed and stared at the dark stains on the floor in front of the mirror. *Blood,* she thought.

Cindy crawled around the kitchen bar and made her way to the front door. She grabbed the doorknob and pulled herself up to her feet, then she fastened the deadbolt.

Click.

The noise made Charlotte flinch. Her shoulders stayed hunched up next to her ears. She turned around slowly, as if she were expecting to find someone pointing a gun at her.

"Charlotte," Cindy said. "Don't scream."

Gazing at her friend with awe and disbelief, Charlotte's eyes got bigger and bigger. Her mouth opened and closed, opened and closed, and opened and closed again, as if she were giving a speech—but no sound came out. The plastic bag fell from her hand. All of the bags rustled on the floor next to her feet. The icy milkshake slid across her hand as she trembled.

"Holy shit," she whispered.

Cindy's condition had worsened since she called Charlotte. Loose, gooey skin—completely covered in bruises and rashes—dangled from every part of her body. It looked like she was wearing an oversized costume of human skin. There were bald spots all around her head, hair plucked out like dandelions from a garden.

Charlotte stuttered, "Is–Is that bah... bluh... *blood* on your lips?"

Cindy nodded and raised her right hand, revealing the bloodied paper towel wrapped around her mutilated finger. She didn't have to say a word. Charlotte got the message loud and clear: *Autocannibalism.* Cindy lifted her shirt up and revealed the plugged wound on her stomach. To show Charlotte the extent of her problem, she scratched her breast with her good index finger.

She effortlessly peeled a thin strip of skin off the outer side of her breast. The skin spiraled to the floor like the shavings of a sharpened pencil.

Eyes flooded with tears, Charlotte asked, "What happened to you?"

With a forced smile, shaky and insincere, Cindy said, "You remember that 'miracle' capsule I told you about? Well, they worked too well."

"Pills... Pills did this to you?"

"Yes. And now I need to eat *a lot* or whatever I put in my body is going to *eat me* from inside. Please tell me you brought everything I ordered."

"Ye–Yeah, it's... it's right here."

"Thank you. Thank you so much."

Cindy hobbled towards her. Charlotte held the milkshake out in front of her and stepped back, trying to keep her distance. Keeping her head down, Cindy took the milkshake and grabbed the plastic bag, then she brought the food to the kitchen table. Charlotte remained in the living room, immobilized by her fear.

Charlotte stood in the kitchen archway, concerned about her friend and afraid for her own safety. Cindy devoured the food like a feral animal. She took giant bites of the burgers, even eating some of the wrapping paper with it. She jammed fistfuls of French fries and onion rings slathered with ketchup into her mouth. And she put it all down with big swigs of her milkshake.

"Is it, um... Is it enough?" Charlotte asked, her voice

wavering. Cindy didn't hear her over all of her munching and gulping. Charlotte coughed, then said, "Cindy, is it enough food? Are you going to be okay now?"

Cindy swallowed loudly. Barbecue sauce, ketchup, and blood stained her lips. She leaned back in her seat and lifted her shirt. Her skin was the same—loose, bruised, rosy. She gasped as the loose skin on her belly rippled. She saw green veins slithering across her breasts and abdomen, too, as if there were snakes under her skin.

Although Charlotte couldn't see it, Cindy could *feel* her body changing. A feeling of warmth—*painful* warmth—spread through her torso as her skin moved and organs shifted.

She said, "I think I bought some time, but I don't know how much. I need more food."

"You need an ambulance."

"I don't even know what's wrong with me."

"But you know you need food. That's what you've been saying. So, if we take you to a hospital, then they can give you, like, a feeding tube or an IV or something like that."

"Charlotte, look at me. I'm a monster."

"You're not a–"

"It took you five minutes to get closer to me and you're still too scared to get close. And you're my best friend. Imagine what everyone else would think of me. I can't just call an ambulance. They'd... They'd quarantine me. They'd rather let me die alone than help me. That's the way it's always been in my life. You wouldn't understand because you're not a monster... because you're not me."

Charlotte sniffled and looked up at the ceiling to stop her tears from streaming across her face. She could feel Cindy's pain and sadness. Crying, Cindy took a bite of a burger and shoved another fistful of fries into her mouth.

Charlotte said, "But you won't be alone because I'll be with you. And they can't quarantine you in your apartment if I drive you to the hospital, right? I can be with you every step of the way if you let me help you."

Cindy swallowed her food and looked at Charlotte. She saw an angel standing in her kitchen archway. The apartment looked brighter when she was around. Charlotte snickered as tears ran down her face.

She said, "I was already your Uber Eats driver, right? Might as well be your personal ambulance, too."

Cindy said, "I can't go out looking like this. I just... *I can't*, okay?"

"Don't be like that, Cin. You said it yourself: This is a life-or-death situation. I know it's hard, but this isn't the time to worry about your appearance."

"I know, but... I don't know why, but I just can't stop thinking about it. I'm scared of what people are going to say about me because of the way I look. It hurts. Their words always hurt."

"I won't let them hurt you. By the time you get into

the emergency room, you'll be around people who only care about your health anyway. We can even cover you up a little bit."

Charlotte grabbed a long, hooded coat and a hair tie from the top of the dresser. Then she crouched and picked up a pair of sandals from the floor near the bed. She stopped in the crouch position upon spotting the trail of blood on the carpet. She feared Cindy was going to die without immediate medical assistance.

She went back to the kitchen with the clothes and said, "Put this on. I'll tie your hair in a bun, then you can cover your head with the hood. No one will see your face or body until we're at the hospital. I can promise you that. And once we're there, the doctors won't care about your appearance. They're there to help, not judge. Okay?"

As Charlotte styled her hair, Cindy said, "Just promise you won't leave me alone. Even if the doctors say you can't come in with me, tell them that you *have* to. Force your way through."

"I won't leave your side. You have my word. Now, come on, let's get going, hon. You can lean on me if you need some help."

Charlotte grabbed Cindy's waist and helped her stand up. Arm in arm, they staggered out of the apartment. Cindy kept her head down to hide her face. Only able to see the floor and her feet, she put all of her trust in Charlotte to lead her to recovery.

12

THE DRIVE

"YOU HAVE TO HELP ME OUT HERE, OKAY?" CHARLOTTE said as she tightened her grip on Cindy's arm and hoisted her up. They moved down a hallway on the first floor of the apartment building. Charlotte said, "I'm parked right outside in the alley. If you want to... to get through this, you have to fight. Work with me, hon."

Cindy limped next to Charlotte, dragging her feet like a child dragged to a clothing store. Her ankles stung, her calves cramped and relaxed one at a time, and her thighs ached. She grunted and groaned with each painful step. Her eyelids flickered as her vision adjusted to the bright fluorescent light in the corridor. She saw the finish line in front of them—two glass doors leading to darkness.

"I'm... trying," she said weakly. "It hurts... so much."

"I know, I know. But you have to keep going. I'm

sorry, but I can't carry you on my own. I need your help. We're so close. Don't give up."

"I'm... I'm trying."

Cindy bit her bottom lip and breathed deeply through her nose as she leaned away from Charlotte. She tried to walk on her own, wobbling with each slow, heavy step. Charlotte put her arm around Cindy's waist and helped her reach the end of the hallway. Cindy could feel the meddlesome neighbors peeking out at them from their peepholes

One middle-aged guy cracked his door open for a better view while keeping his security chain fastened. He was just nosy, not helpful.

As they pushed the doors open at the end of the hall, Cindy screamed and teetered. Charlotte glanced back at her and gasped. Over half of Cindy's lower lip dangled over her chin. She had unintentionally bitten through her lip while exerting herself. Trails of blood ran down her chin and neck. Her lower gums and teeth, glazed with blood, were exposed even when her mouth was closed. Her teeth hadn't deteriorated like the rest of her body.

Cindy could see the damage through her reflection on the door. She put her hand over her mouth and placed some pressure on her butchered lip, as if trying to reattach it. Her touch only worsened the pain, though. On the verge of collapsing, she squealed and swayed. Charlotte placed her palms on Cindy's cheeks and examined her face. The grisly wound made her sick and left her at a loss for words. So, she hugged Cindy. They sniveled in the doorway for about a minute.

While gently patting the back of Cindy's head, Charlotte said, "It's okay. You're going to be okay. You just have to... Just try not to touch yourself anymore, okay?"

"Just get me the hell outta here," Cindy replied, nodding and sniffling.

"Just give me a second, okay? Just one second. I want to make sure everything's good for the ride."

Ass Charlotte hurried to the black sedan parked in the alley, Cindy stepped out of the building and stared up at the dark sky—no stars in sight. It was an unusually calm night.

"Peace for everyone but me," she whispered.

Cindy turned her attention to Charlotte. Her friend took a large blue beach towel from the trunk and draped it over the back seat, obviously trying to stop Cindy from dirtying her car.

As she approached the car, Cindy asked, "Are you rolling out the red carpet just for me?"

Charlotte stopped her frantic movements and glanced over at her. Cindy smiled, which caused her lower lip to detach a little more. She didn't appear to feel any pain, though. Big drops of blood fell from her mouth and plopped on the pavement.

"I guess it's more like a *blue* carpet," she said.

"N–No, that's not... Don't get the wrong idea. I just thought it would keep you warm and comfortable."

"You didn't just clean your car, didn't you? It looks sparkling clean to me. I thought I saw you post something up about it on Instagram or Twitter or Facebook or whatever *bullshit* social media site we all hate but can't stop using. You did, right?"

"I did, but that's not why I'm doing this. Maybe I should have asked you first. I'm sorry if I was insensitive."

"Nothing to be sorry about. I'm just messing with you. And even if you did put that towel there because you didn't want me to get your car dirty–"

"I didn't."

"–I probably would have done the same if I were in your position. So, can I sit now? I feel like my legs are going to snap."

Charlotte stood in silence for a moment. She was unnerved by Cindy's sudden shifts in attitude. One moment, she was sobbing due to her bitten lip. The next, she was walking on her own and hurling snide remarks.

"Sure," Charlotte said. "Hop in. Get some rest."

As Cindy settled into the back seat, moving with an abundance of caution, Charlotte sat in the driver's seat and buckled herself in. She watched her friend through the rearview mirror.

"Need some help?" she asked

"I'm... fine."

"What about your seat belt?"

"My ribs hurt, Char. If I put it on, I think they might break as soon as we hit the first red light. Just go."

"I can drive slo–"

"Just go. *Please*."

Charlotte sighed. She could only hope the drunks were still at the bars and the potholes were finally filled in the city. The engine purred as they drove off.

Eyes on the road, Charlotte said, "Let me know if you need me to slow down or pull over. I'll try to get you there as quickly as possible. It'll probably take about fifteen or twenty minutes."

"Don't worry about me," Cindy said from behind Charlotte. She was leaning against the door and staring out the window. She said, "I won't puke on your seats. I promise I won't make this night any worse for you."

"It's not about that. I just want to make sure you're okay."

"I have no idea if I'm going to be okay. I mean, do you... do you really think they can help me?"

Charlotte said, "I've never seen anything like this before. But I'm *sure* they can help you. They know what they're doing. They're trained for this. And if it's as simple as putting food into your body like you said it was, then I'm positive you'll be fine. Try not to think too much about it right now. Stress won't do your body any favors. It never does."

"You're probably right."

The car rolled to a stop at a red light. Five cars drove through the intersection. The other drivers appeared to be on their best behavior—no speeding, no swerving, no texting.

Charlotte drummed her fingers on the steering wheel and stared out the windshield, lost in her thoughts. Cindy's pained groaning and growling behind her made her skin crawl.

The light turned green.

Charlotte drove forward and asked, "What really happened to you, Cindy? How is this even possible?"

"It was the 'miracle' capsules. I didn't know what was in them. I just knew they burned fat. No... They *ate* fat. And they really worked. They worked so damn well. I know you couldn't believe it when you saw me at your wedding reception. I lost over a hundred pounds. And that... that made me feel better about myself. I felt like one of you."

"One of... me?"

"Like a... *a person.*"

Tears stung Charlotte's eyes. She wanted to comfort Cindy, but she feared it was too late to help her. She made a right turn and kept driving.

She said, "So, you don't know what was in those capsules. What are we supposed to tell the doctors? How do we stop or reverse the side effects? Hmm? How do we stop you from... from melting or whatever's happening to you?"

"I spoke to the man who sold them to me. His name is Deki. Hideki."

"Is that a first name?" Charlotte asked, shrugging. "A last name? A nickname?"

"I really don't know. He was just... so handsome. And kind, too. I thought he was one of those 'player' types, but he was actually very sweet. I would... I would really like to date him in the future. Yeah, that would be nice..."

Cindy looked up at the ceiling of the car and giggled deliriously. She entered a frenzied, dreamlike state. Charlotte glanced over her shoulder, baffled by her strange laughter.

"Snap out of it," she said. The laughter continued. Charlotte honked the horn, then said, "Cindy, talk to me. How do we stop it? How do we save you?"

Cindy's giggling softened to a snicker. She said, "I have to eat. That's all the advice he gave me. 'Eat or be eaten.' If I don't eat... Well, you get the picture."

"Goddammit, Cindy. Why would you take something like that? Huh? Why would you take something that could potentially *kill* you? *Why?*"

Cindy had a hundred excuses ready to go, but only the truth stood out in her mind: *Because I'm insecure.*

She said, "They weren't supposed to be deadly. I just didn't follow the instructions. Didn't eat enough, y'know? I was supposed to be stuffing my face while I took the capsules, but I didn't. This was my fault and I can't blame anyone else. I know that." She looked out the passenger window and said, "If the hospital thing doesn't work out, maybe we should visit Deki. He could help me, right? I remember he said he made the capsules, so he should know how to stop this."

"I guess so. You think he might have, like, an antidote or something? Knowing these type of scumbag 'entrepreneurs,' he'll probably try to sell it to you. But if it exists and it works, it'll be worth every penny."

Cindy nodded. She thought about Deki, her knight in shining armor. She felt safe around him. She pictured herself—her healthy, lean self—lying in bed with him on a warm sunny morning. Her fantasy felt like a memory. Then her face stiffened and she stopped nodding. A different knight—*a bigger one*—galloped across her mind.

"Stop the car," she said.

"What?" Charlotte responded. "What's wrong? You going to puke or–"

Cindy moaned as she leaned towards the center console. She grabbed Charlotte's shoulder and said, "Stop the car and give me your phone. We have to go to Joseph's house. I have to call him. Have to... to warn him."

"*Warn him?* What are you talking about?"

"I gave him some of those capsules weeks ago and I haven't heard from him since. If he took them and he didn't follow the instructions..."

"Then he could be like you," Charlotte said.

"Or worse. He could be dead. I need to check on him. Give me your phone, Charlotte, and turn this thing around. We have to help him."

"Okay! Okay!" Charlotte yelled as she made a U-turn. She passed her cell phone to Cindy and said, "I hope he's okay. Please let him be okay..."

13

BODILY FLUIDS

CHARLOTTE PARKED NEXT TO A TWO-STORY TOWNHOUSE
—*Joseph's home*. Cindy crawled to the other side of the
back seat and peered through the passenger window.
The porch lights were on while the windows were
dark. The residents were fast asleep. The streets and
alleys around the townhouse were empty and quiet.
Although she didn't detect any signs of trouble, a bad
feeling festered in Cindy's gut. It was the calm before
the storm.

"I'm sorry, Joseph," she whispered. "I should have
never done this."

Charlotte said, "Hey, don't overthink it. You know
Joseph. He probably didn't even take 'em. He might
just be sleeping."

"I called him five times, Char. He sleeps like a bear,
but he's not hibernating. No, I think... I think he's hurt.
He's hurt because of me."

"Because of those 'miracle' capsules, Cindy, not because of you. You didn't make them."

"But I gave them to him. He didn't even ask me for them. I gave them to him because *I* wanted him to change with me. This is all my fault. I caused this because I'm so damn stupid and so damn selfish. What is wrong with me?"

Like an angry parent scolding her child, Charlotte turned to face the back seat, wagged her index finger at Cindy, and said, "*Stop it*. Don't talk like that. It won't do you or him any good. We're just wasting valuable time here. Let's stop thinking and start doing, okay?"

"Yeah, you... you're totally right," Cindy said. She wiped her eyes with her sleeve and said, "We have to check up on him. I have to save him."

Charlotte exited the vehicle first, then she helped Cindy climb out. She led Cindy to Unit B. The one-story home was attached to two two-story units in the townhouse. On her way to the front door, Cindy covered her head with the hood of her coat. She knew Joseph loved her unconditionally, but if he didn't take the capsules and suffer from the same side effects, she didn't want him to see her in her current condition.

Charlotte rang the doorbell. She waited ten seconds, then rang it again. After ten seconds of silence, she knocked on the door five times, pounding away at it with the bottom of her fist.

There was no answer.

"He might not be home," Charlotte said. "I think

he's been entertaining family for the past few weeks. His brother came to town around the time of my wedding, remember?"

"Joe's car is in his parking space and his brother was supposed to leave over a week ago."

"I heard his brother stuck around a little longer than he was expecting. He posted about it on Facebook. Maybe he's still here. Maybe they took his car and went out for drinks."

"I have to be sure," Cindy said as she stepped to the side.

"What are you doing? Wait, let me..."

Charlotte's voice tapered off as she watched her friend. One leg at a time, Cindy got down to her knees while facing the bush next to the porch. She pushed a stone aside, then used her cupped hands to sweep the dirt. She avoided digging because she didn't want to lose another fingertip. Yet, the simple sweeping action made her hands and arms ache. Gasping and whining and trembling, she fought through the pain. It took her a minute to find Joseph's spare key.

She handed it to Charlotte and said, "Take it."

Charlotte was mesmerized by Cindy's endurance and determination. She took the key, then helped Cindy to her feet. She frowned as she caught a glimpse of the loose skin accumulating around Cindy's ankles. It had turned black and coarse. It looked like she was wearing melted GPS ankle bracelets on each leg.

With one arm wrapped around Cindy's waist,

Charlotte opened the door. The hinges *creaked*, announcing their arrival. Light from the porch poured into the home. Cindy grimaced while Charlotte pinched her nose with her free hand. A foul stench, like rotten eggs blended with fresh feces, blew through the doorway.

"Christ, what is that smell?" Charlotte asked.

"It doesn't matter. We just have to find Joseph," Cindy said. As they entered the home, Cindy shouted, "Joseph! Joseph, it's Cindy!"

"And Charlotte! Joseph, you in here?!"

"Talk to me, baby! Say something!"

Again, there was no answer. The friends stood in the living room. There was a large plastic bowl, opened bags of potato chips, and empty beer cans on the table between the television and sofa. The Mexican serape on the sofa had dark stains on it. The kitchen was seamlessly connected to the living room, only defined by the change from carpet to linoleum flooring. There was an empty pizza box on the dining table and dirty plates in the sink.

There were no signs of Joseph or his brother.

"His room is over there," Cindy said as she pointed at the hallway next to the kitchen. "He has to be sleeping. Maybe he's wearing headphones. Maybe he's, um... Maybe..."

"Let's go see. Come on, work with me, Cin. I can't carry you on my own."

Wheezing and groaning, they lumbered down the

hallway. Cindy glanced at the first door to her right and shook her head. She wasn't expecting to find her boyfriend hiding in a puny storage closet. They stopped on the second door to the right.

"Is this it?" Charlotte asked.

"It's the bathroom."

"You... have to go?"

Cindy said, "No. But maybe he's in there." She laughed feebly, then said, "He spends a lot of time in there."

Charlotte looked at the gap under the door and said, "The light's off. I don't think anyone's in there."

"No. Someone's definitely in there."

"What? How do you know that?"

"I can smell him."

Charlotte sneered as she sniffed. The stench of rot was stronger there. Cindy opened the door. Cheeks inflated, Charlotte let go of her and put her hands over her mouth. The awful smell attacked her nostrils and brought tears to her eyes. Unable to see anything, Cindy flicked the light switch. Her eyes bugging out, she was struck with a bout of dizziness. She leaned on the doorframe to stop herself from falling. Charlotte tottered back until she crashed into the wall behind her.

The toilet was filled to the brim with a maroon sludge. The mirror on the medicine cabinet was cracked. Underneath it, the sink and neighboring countertop were smeared with dried blood. The shower curtain hung from the rod on two rings. The rest of the rings had been snapped off. Blood stained the curtain, the side of the bathtub, and the floor, too. It had dried in the grooves between the tiles.

There was a *mass* of liquefied human flesh in the bathtub. Discolored skin, broken bones, yellow layers of thick fat, and patches of bushy black hair floated in the crimson liquid—a nasty concoction of bodily fluids, mostly consisting of blood. A few fingers, a foot, a skinless thigh, and an eyeball bobbed around at the surface of the liquid like buoys in the ocean.

The body was still melting, causing the fluids and pieces to drift this way and that way.

"No, no, no, no, no," Cindy said as she limped into the bathroom. She stopped between the toilet and bathtub. Staring down at the liquefied body, she cried, "Joseph, no... Oh my God, I'm so sorry. It–It wasn't supposed to be like–like... like *this*. I didn't mean to hurt you. I just wanted us to–to be perfect. I wanted us to be... to be like everyone else."

Charlotte returned to the doorway, weeping and shuddering. She was rendered speechless by the grotesque scene. She knew people could be burned to ashes, but she had never seen an entire human body *melt* like that. She couldn't make any sense of it. She thought about calling 911, but she couldn't think of what to say.

Cindy got down to her knees in front of the tub and examined the liquefied remains. She felt like vomiting

—partly thanks to the stomach-churning gore before her and partly due to the debilitating grief within her.

Through the layers of loose skin and fat folded over fat, she had trouble identifying each body part. Some fingers and a foot stuck out of the bodily fluids at one end of the bathtub, and a hand and some toes protruded from the liquid on the other side of it. A man's flabby breast rose to the surface. She hooked her finger around the plug's chain and moved it aside for a better view of it. Blood running down it, dripping from the nipple like milk from a teat, she noticed the ink on the breast.

As Cindy leaned closer to the tub, Charlotte said, "Cin, don't."

"It's not him," Cindy said.

"Just get away from there."

"It's not him."

"Cindy, please! We need to take you to the hospital and I need to go to the police. Someone has to report this!"

Cindy looked at her and said, "This isn't Joseph. Joe, he doesn't have any tattoos. This... This has to be his brother." As she leaned away from the tub, finger still curled around the chain, she said, "Joseph must have shared the capsules with him. So, maybe he's still..."

Clunk! The noise came from the bathtub as she accidentally removed the plug. It was followed by a *gurgling* sound as the tub drained. The bodily fluids sloshed while waves of fat and skin clashed. Cindy stood up and stepped back, horrified. A severed penis rose to the top of the human slush under the faucet. A droopy face, drenched in blood, surfaced next to it, then sank back into the bodily fluids.

Cindy couldn't put a name to the face, although she had met Joseph's brother many times before. People didn't look the same when their faces weren't attached to their skulls.

With another loud *clunk*, the pipe was clogged and the tub stopped draining. The women stood in awed silence. After about a minute, Cindy limped out of the bathroom. She turned off the light and closed the door behind her.

In a quiet but steady voice, she said, "Joseph's room is down the hall. He has to be there. Let's go."

Leaning against the wall, she moved forward. She only cared about herself and Joseph. With both hands over her mouth, Charlotte kept staring at the bathroom door. She couldn't move on as easily as Cindy— couldn't just shrug off the *melted* body in the bathtub. She took another minute to collect herself, then she reluctantly followed Cindy's lead.

Standing in front of the door at the end of the hall, Cindy clenched her jaw and grasped the doorknob. She tasted the blood gushing from her weak gums. She was used to it, though. She turned the knob and pushed the door open. Standing next to her, Charlotte gaped at the bedroom. Her hands went back to her mouth as she retched. Cindy could only cry, bloody spittle spurting out from between her gritted teeth.

Across from the door, there was a king-sized bed under a window. The rolling closet doors to the right were stamped with bloody handprints. Directly to the left of the door, there was a dresser with a large flatscreen television on top. The television was tuned to a muted news broadcast. The blue glow from the TV illuminated most of the room.

Another massive pile of liquefying flesh was on the bed. Loose skin covered the mattress like a blanket. It even hung from the edges of the bed. It was bruised and red all over. A large pair of torn boxers was tangled in the soft meat. His belly appeared to be swirling and bubbling, like stew in a cauldron. The capsules had weakened his bones, so he could barely move.

There were holes, as small as fingertips and as big as fists, across his chest. His bloody ribs were left exposed. His intercostal muscles—the muscles between his ribs—were fizzing like soda, blood frothing over the bones. His hair had fallen out. His cheeks were torn to shreds, the inside of his mouth visible through the remaining strings of skin. His nose was gone. He swallowed it after it had slid into his mouth.

Cindy couldn't identify him through his body, but

she recognized his eyes. Despite all of his suffering, there was a gentle, understanding look in his eyes.

"Joseph," Cindy said.

"Cin... Cin... Cindy," Joseph responded, speaking slowly in a thick, raspy voice. He was sitting up in bed, propped up by a couple of pillows. He said, "Is... that... you?"

Shedding tears of regret and misery, Cindy walked to the foot of the bed and nodded. Charlotte stayed behind, frozen with fear. A gurgling sound came out of Joseph's mouth. Some of the remaining strands of skin on his cheeks tore as he attempted to smile. It looked and sounded like he was trying to laugh.

"It's been... a while," he said. "You look... beautiful... babe. A real... angel. I'm so... proud of you."

Cindy cried harder as she gazed into her boyfriend's eyes. The skin on his forehead was starting to droop over his eyes, partially obscuring his vision. *He doesn't know what he's saying*, she thought. *Doesn't know what he's seeing.* She was amazed by his attitude. Despite the disturbing circumstances, he was as optimistic and romantic as ever.

"Thank you, hon–honey" she said, voice shaking. Trying to act normal, she smiled and said, "What, um... What have you been up to?"

"You know... just livin'."

"How do you... feel?"

"Like... a million bucks."

Joseph tried to laugh again. Slimy blood oozed out

from the slits on his cheeks. Cindy couldn't help but sob. Charlotte was crying now, too, her legs shaking uncontrollably.

"What happened to you?" Cindy asked.

Joseph said, "I did it. I took... the diet pills. Two... or three... on the first week. And it..." He coughed, sending blood trickling out of every hole on his head —his mouth, his nose holes, his ear canals, his eye sockets. Wheezing with each pause, he said, "And it... didn't work out. I didn't see any results. I was going to... give up. But I didn't want to disappoint you, Cin. So, I... I gave a few to my brother... and we started to work through it together. You know... to get motivated. No junk food, just the gym and the pills... but we just got worse. We gave up and started eating junk again, but... it just kept getting worse, babe. I'm sorry."

"No, this was *not* your fault, Joseph. I should have given you more instructions, more warnings... more love. I pushed you into this. It's my fault. I messed up. I'm the one who should be sorry. Not you."

Joseph shook his head at her. He felt her regret and sorrow. Even in his misshapen, anguished state, he couldn't blame her for anything. He didn't want her to feel any more pain. Despite Cindy's inconsistent love, Joseph's fondness for her remained strong and pure.

He said, "Don't... blame yourself. *I* decided to take those... things. It was *my* choice, not yours. Besides, it's... not as bad as it looks. I think I found the problem,

Cin. You gotta eat or... or *this* happens to you. You have... to... eat."

"I know, I know. I was coming here to tell you that. We're going to the hospital now. We can get a feeding tube or something like that. I think it'll keep us alive. We might have to call an ambulance for you, but we–"

Joseph unleashed an awful, gurgling scream as he lifted his arms from the bed. Before Cindy could say another word, he dug his thick fingers into his bubbling stomach. He grabbed a fistful of loose skin in each hand, then he moved his hands away from each other. His fat stretched like hot cheese on a fresh pizza before his flesh tore with a *shredding* sound, leaving a gaping hole at the center of his abdomen.

"Joseph!" Cindy bellowed.

Charlotte knew the worst was yet to come. People didn't disembowel themselves just for the sake of it. She entered the room and tugged on Cindy's shoulder.

"We have to go," she said quickly. "Cindy, we can't watch this! We have to get help! Come on, let's go!"

Cindy yelled, "Joseph, stop!"

Joseph unfurled his fists. The globs of fat landed on the blanket of skin around him with *splat* sounds. He lowered his hands into the hole on his stomach. His abdominal muscles were gone, so he had easy access to his organs. He pulled a section of his small intestine out. It fell over his lap. His face twisted up in an ugly, inhuman knot as terrible bolts of pain blasted through him from his abdomen.

He said, "You have to... eat... or you'll die. Promise me... you'll eat, Cindy." He laughed for a few seconds, then he started coughing. He said, "I know... you don't like to eat, but you have to–to... to do it. I want you... to be healthy... to stay alive. You deserve... to be happy, baby. I love you so much."

"I love you, too, Joseph," Cindy said.

"Joseph, don't do it!" Charlotte cried as she pulled Cindy towards the door. "I'll get you to the hospital! I'll get you an ambulance! Just please wait a minute!"

"We have to eat," Joseph whispered as he eyed his bloody intestine.

He raised the organ to his chin, pulling more of it out of his abdomen. Along with a deep, raspy breath, he slurped the intestine into his mouth like ramen. He felt it in his mouth, but he couldn't taste it due to all of the blood that was already in there. He bit into it with his remaining teeth, then shook his head frantically, like a dog playing with a chew toy.

He tore a piece of the intestine off. He chewed the thick, durable piece for a few seconds, then swallowed it.

He said, "It's not... that bad. Meaty... a little sour... I'd taste better with some barbecue sauce. I have some... in the kitchen."

"Joseph, stop it!" Charlotte pleaded.

Hugging Cindy from behind, she had managed to drag her friend into the hallway. Joseph rocked from side to side, like a turtle stuck on his back. He scooted to the edge of the mattress, dragging the blanket of loose skin behind him. He dropped his legs off the bed, then pushed himself up to his feet. A wave of blood and guts poured out of the hole on his abdomen.

His intestines, small and large, hung from the wound, dangling close to his knees. His spleen, stomach, and pancreas fell to the floor. After he had disemboweled himself, a powerful numbness spread across his torso. He didn't feel the organs slip out, but he could see them clearly. He knew he was falling apart —*dying*—but he kept a semblance of control in order to instill a sense of confidence in Cindy.

He kept fighting so Cindy wouldn't give up. He didn't want to admit defeat, either. He was determined to get some sauce for his meal.

"I'm so sorry," Cindy whimpered.

As he took an unsteady step towards the door, Joseph's right leg *snapped*. It was bent like a boomerang at the center, sticking out to his right. His femur and tibia bones cut through his skin and stuck out of his leg like large, sharp shards. He screamed and swayed as he struggled to keep his balance, unwittingly causing his protruding bones to saw through his flesh. Blood sprinkled in a circular motion, spraying out at the bed, the nightstand, the closet door, and the floor in front of the women. Within seconds, his leg was cut in half at the kneecap.

He plummeted to the floor, a cape of skin following

behind him. His right foot remained firmly planted on the carpet.

Cindy gasped, then yelled, "Joseph, no!"

Charlotte stopped her from stumbling back into the room. She cared about Joseph, but she feared he was a lost cause. She focused on saving Cindy from suffering the same fate.

She said, "We have to go."

"Let go of me! Let me help him!"

"You can't."

"He needs me!"

"It's too fucking late, Cindy! If we don't get you help —*real help*—you'll end up like him! I know it hurts, sweetie, I know it does, but we *can't* stay here. We can't!"

Joseph lifted his head from the floor and looked over at the doorway. He couldn't see a thing because the skin on his forehead had slid over his eyes.

He said, "Get out... Cindy. I'll... I'll see you later. I love... I love you."

"I love you, too, Joseph," Cindy said. "I love you so much."

She took one final glance at her boyfriend as Charlotte dragged her away from the room. Like his brother, he had been reduced to a huge heap of liquefied flesh. For the first time since the beginning of their relationship, she saw beyond his figure. She saw his generous, soft-hearted soul. She wanted to remember him for his kindness. Positive memories of their relationship poured into her mind.

"I'm sorry," she whispered as she was dragged out of the home, forced to abandon the only man who truly ever loved her.

14

THE CURE

SITTING IN THE PASSENGER SEAT OF CHARLOTTE'S SEDAN, Cindy stared at the fast-food restaurant in front of her —a 24-hour Jack in the Box. The strip mall behind the Jack in the Box was desolate and dark while the surrounding streets were lit up by dim streetlamps. In the restaurant, patrons—from teenaged to elderly— satisfied their cravings for greasy burgers and curly fries. The chatter from the teenagers could be heard from the parking lot. It was a garble of noise, but Cindy believed she was hearing every single word from their mouths.

'*What's wrong with her?*'

'*She looks sick.*'

'*She's disgusting!*'

Then the overlapping voices turned into hysterical laughter. But none of the patrons looked her way. They were unaware of her existence.

Cindy sank in her seat and pulled the hood of her coat over her forehead to hide her face. Despite the escalating situation, her insecurities continued to eat away at her mind. A crippling fear of death haunted her as well. She waited in the car because she was afraid to move. She kept replaying Joseph's deterioration in her head. *It could happen to me,* she thought. *It IS happening to me. I'm next. I'm going to die like him if I don't stop this.*

The driver door swung open, but she didn't react. She kept her eyes on the restaurant, watching the patrons through the tall windows.

"I brought the food," Charlotte said as she sat in the driver's seat.

She had a brown bag in one hand and a cardboard drink carrier with two milkshakes in the other. The brown bag was so full that it looked like it was about to tear open.

Charlotte asked, "Did you hear me?" She put a milkshake in each cupholder on the center console, then she closed the door behind her. She opened the bag up and said, "Burgers, chicken nuggets, curly fries, onion rings, tacos... I tried to get a little of everything. It should be enough to buy us some time. The hospital's about ten minutes away. Maybe less if the streets stay empty like this."

From under her hood, Cindy continued to gaze at the restaurant. She hadn't said a word to Charlotte since they left Joseph's apartment. The tragedy—*the guilt*—had rendered her mute.

Charlotte said, "Cindy, you *have* to eat. Please, I don't..." Her voice broke, causing her to pause and grunt. She sighed, then said, "I don't want to lose you, too."

Cindy continued to brood over Joseph's death. The little voice in her head was telling her to give up and join him. *You'd be happier if you were dead,* it said. But a part of her wanted to keep fighting. Survival was hardwired in her brain. She reached into the bag and took out a burger and a container of curly fries.

Charlotte watched as Cindy devoured the food, stuffing her mouth with fries, burger, milkshake, and even some wrapping paper all at once. Gulping and slurping and squishing sounds filled the car's interior.

"We should start heading out," Charlotte said. She turned to face forward and put her key in the ignition. She said, "Keep eating and I think you'll be fine. Just let me know if you're feeling sick or if you need more food. I think there's a McDonald's on the way. We can probably use their restroom, too, if you need it."

"Wait," Cindy said, mouth full of food.

She touched Charlotte's wrist, stopping her from turning the key in the ignition. Charlotte looked at her curiously, surprised to hear her raspy voice again.

Cindy swallowed her food, then said, "Let's wait here for a second. I need to think."

Charlotte responded, "Think about what, Cin?

There's nothing else to think about. You saw what happened to Joseph and his brother. Let's just go to the hospital. The doctors will take care of you. You'll get better and this... this *nightmare* will finally end. And I'll be right there with you. Seriously, I just saw Joseph... I– I saw..." Her voice broke again. This time, she needed a few more seconds to clear her throat and moisten her mouth. Voice trembling, she said, "I saw some messed-up shit tonight, but I'm still here. I can't watch you hurt yourself like Joseph did. *I can't.*"

"The hospital is... useless. Doctors can't save me. They won't be able to–to... *identify* whatever is happening to me. They've probably never seen anything like this before. I mean, I'm fucking *melting* for crying out loud, Char. You know what they're going to do to me? They'll put me on some feeding tube, then watch me. Observe and take notes. That's it. I'll be nothing more than a medical experiment to them. Really, what can they do to stop this? Hmm? What can they do, Charlotte?"

"Calm down, Cindy. Everything–"

"Don't tell me to calm down!" Cindy barked. "Don't tell me everything is going to be okay when it *isn't*. We both know that. Stop talking to me like I'm a damn child. Stop patronizing me! Just stop it!"

Charlotte leaned away from her, startled by Cindy's hostility. She gave her a minute to collect herself, then she leaned closer to her and caressed her forehead, pushing her thinning hair away. Cindy shuddered at her touch. She could feel Charlotte's kindness and understanding. The reaction confused her. *How can she be so caring after my tantrum?* she thought.

Cindy took another big bite from her burger as she cried, her tears sogging up the bun. She took two more bites. Then red blotches appeared at the bottom of her vision. She looked down at the burger and saw red in the meat and bun. She assumed it was ketchup, then she felt another tear fall from her face. It landed on the bun—and it was red. She heard Charlotte gasp next to her.

Cindy examined her reflection in the rearview mirror. Bloody tears leaked from her red eyes. She dropped the burger and started rocking back and forth. Terrifying thoughts ran through her mind: *My brain is bleeding. My brain is MELTING. I'm dying.*

Although shaking and whining, Charlotte bolted into action. She knew she had to act to stop Cindy from panicking. She grabbed a napkin from the bag and dabbed Cindy's face with it, removing the blood from her eyes and nose. Then she crumpled the napkin and tossed it in the back seat along with Cindy's half-eaten burger. She handed her a crunchy taco instead.

"We have to go," Charlotte said.

"I told you, I can't go to the hospital. They'd just chain me up like an animal."

"They'll feed you. They'll give you an IV. I'm sure of it."

"Then what? What if that doesn't work? They're not just going to let me walk out of there. I'd just be putting myself in a corner."

"So, what do *you* want to do? Hmm? You want me to watch you die? You want to melt in my car? Is that it?"

"No. I want you to help me."

"That's what I'm trying to–"

"Charlotte, listen to me," Cindy interrupted. "I don't know what is in those capsules and I don't have any on me right now. They're all gone. How am I going to explain this to a doctor? 'Give me all of your food. I have to eat or I'll be eaten from the inside.' You think a bunch of doctors are going to listen to that? No. It won't work. I have to find the man who sold them to me. I need to go to Deki."

Charlotte huffed. She turned the key in the ignition, then reversed out of the parking space. Both hands on the steering wheel, she drove out of the parking lot and took a right on the street. Despite Cindy's explanation, she was determined to get her to the hospital. She felt responsible for her survival. She failed to save Joseph, but she wasn't going to let Cindy die on her watch.

Without glancing at her, she said, "Don't be stupid. I know you're just saying that because you don't want to be seen like this. But this is for the better. I don't know a thing about those damn capsules, but I know this is our best chance at saving you. If you keep wasting time, you might end up with irreversible damage or... or worse. I don't want that and I know you don't want that, either."

"You're wrong. I can beat this. I just have to go to the source."

"You're not making any sense. We have to..."

Cindy stopped listening to her. Her arm shaking from the effort, she grabbed the cell phone from the dashboard. Breathing heavily, she looked up at the ceiling and mouthed some words, trying to remember Deki's phone number. Although she didn't have her phone on her, she had spent several nights staring at his contact information, waiting for the perfect opportunity to call him to ask him on a date.

She dialed his number, then put the call on speaker and held the phone up to her mouth. She was afraid her ear would fall off if she touched it with the phone.

After twenty seconds of ringing, Deki, sounding groggy, answered, "Hello?"

"Deki, it–it's me. It's Cindy."

Deki said, "Cin... *Cindy?* It's past midnight already. What are you doing calling me again? And..." He paused and muttered indistinctly as he shuffled around in bed. He asked, "And whose number is this? Where are you calling me from? If you dragged me into some shit, I swear I'm–"

"It's my friend's phone. I need your help."

"Cindy, I don't have time for this. I'm not involved anymore, okay?"

"Just listen to me. I was going to the hospital, but I don't think they'll be able to help me."

"And you're probably right about that. You fucked up."

"I know! Goddammit, don't you think I know that already? I need you to tell me what I'm supposed to do now. How do I stop this?"

Deki said, "We've been through this already. You have to eat. I hope you didn't ignore me again because if you did... then you'd be in some serious trouble. Stop being stupid."

Cindy sighed in disappointment. She glanced at Charlotte, hoping she would step in and help her talk to him. Charlotte kept her eyes on the road, though. She kept heading to the closest hospital.

"I've been eating, but it's not enough," Cindy said. "I need more. The food might be slowing down the side effects, but I still feel sick. I need a real cure. I'll go to the hospital if I have to, but I have to know what was in the capsules first. Please, I'm begging you. I'll do anything. I–I'll pay you another grand. Hell, I'll pay you two or three thousand more. I'll give you anything. Help me, Deki. Please don't let me die like this. I'm scared. I'm so scared..."

Deki could be heard sighing and mumbling through the speaker. He considered all of his options. He didn't want to involve himself in Cindy's situation. If she died, he feared he would be held accountable for her death. But he couldn't abandon her, either. The genuine fear in her voice filled him with sadness. He was blinded by greed, but he had a good heart.

He said, "Come to my apartment for a 'checkup.' I don't know where you are, but I live at the Mosaic Apartments over at Forest Park. Apartment 8D. That's the apartment marked with a 'D' on the eighth floor. Okay?"

"I know the place," Cindy said, a smile blooming on her face. "We're not far. I think we can be there in, like, ten or fifteen minutes. Thank you so much, Deki. I owe you the–"

"I'm willing to check you out, but don't expect me to solve all of your problems, especially if you're too far gone. I don't have a miracle 'cure' here, but maybe— maybe—we can work something out. I'll see you in a little bit."

The call ended.

Although nothing was promised, Cindy was overwhelmed with relief. A comfortable warmth spread through her body. *Hope?* she thought. Eyelids smeared with blood, she glanced at Charlotte with a set of puppy eyes. She couldn't pout due to her detached lip, though. She looked at her hands. The coarse skin on her fingers drooped down to her palms. Still, she clasped her hands together as if she were praying and faced Charlotte again.

"Take me to the Mosaic Apartments," Cindy said. "Please, Char."

"Your best bet is the hospital."

"It's not, and you know it isn't. It's the safest bet, sure, but it isn't our *best* option. Take me to Deki so he can end this."

"Damn it, Cindy, why do you have to make this so complicated for me? Can't you see what you're asking me to do? You really want me to risk your life like this? If something happens to you, I'd have blood on *my* hands."

Cindy leaned closer to her and said, "Please."

Charlotte stopped at a red light and lowered her head. *I'm just the driver,* she thought. *She might die even if I take her to the hospital. Would it still be my fault then?* The red glow in the car turned green as the traffic light changed.

She made a right turn and said, "Fine. The Mosaic is only a mile or so from Saint John's Hospital anyway, right? But I want to make something clear: At the first sign of trouble, I'm dragging you out of there and taking you to the hospital. I don't care what that man says. If he can't help you, we're out of there *and* I'm calling the cops on him."

"Yeah, I hear you," Cindy said as she leaned back in her seat. "Thank you."

"Don't thank me yet, Cindy. Let's just hope we're making the right decision here."

15

DOCTOR DEKI

THE MOSAIC APARTMENTS WERE LOCATED IN AN affluent, gentrified district of the city. The building stood ten stories tall, towering over the neighboring shopping plaza. The Mosaic had resort-style amenities, including a private lounge, a coffee bar, pools and hot tubs, tennis courts, and a fully equipped 24-hour fitness center.

Charlotte parked in front of the building. She leaned forward in her seat and stared up at the lavish tower through the windshield. Most of the apartments were dark, lights off and curtains closed. Yellow shafts of light shone through some of the windows on the eighth floor, though. The lights in the lobby were still on, too.

"This guy must be loaded," Charlotte said as she glanced at Cindy. "How much did you pay for those 'miracle' pills again?"

"They're capsules," Cindy replied. She looked up at the apartments above and said, "And I probably paid him enough to cover half his rent. Probably not even enough for that."

"I wonder how many other people he sold those 'capsules' to. He must have some sort of scheme going on to afford a place like this. You think his other customers got out of this without the side effects?"

"Only Deki has the answers. Let's go talk to him and get this over with. Can you give me a hand?"

Charlotte was happy to help. She assisted Cindy out of the car, then held her waist and led her into the building's lobby. There was a reception desk to their left, a sitting area directly ahead, and an elevator bank to the right. The lobby had shiny marble flooring and scarlet walls. Through the floor-to-ceiling windows in the sitting area, they could see a group of people laughing and splashing around in an illuminated pool.

"I thought there would be a receptionist or a doorman to greet us," Charlotte said.

Scowling, Cindy said, "That whore receptionist is probably out there skinny-dipping with those guys. Stupid slut..."

Charlotte squinted and tilted her head to the side upon hearing Cindy's unwarranted insults and seeing the anger in her bloodshot eyes. She looked over at the pool. She didn't see any clear signs of a receptionist out there. None of the swimmers were nude, either. *Is she seeing the same thing I'm seeing?* she thought.

She said, "Forget about it. Let's just get on the elevator and head up to this asshole's apartment."

They went into an elevator and hit the button labeled '8.' As they ascended, Charlotte blabbered about the potential consequences of failure. She spoke about her fear of losing her best friend to such a horrible, avoidable sickness. Her feelings were sincere.

But Cindy ignored her. She didn't want Charlotte's sympathy. She only sought results now. With her life on the line, she couldn't be bothered to think about anyone but herself.

She stared at her reflection in the elevator doors, hypnotized by her grotesque appearance. She was still wearing a black coat over a big black t-shirt and a pair of sandals. Detached locks of her hair clung to her clothes like pet fur. Only some blonde patches of hair stuck out of her balding, sagging scalp.

Streaks of dried blood were smeared all over her cheeks. Her bottom lip was barely attached to her face, sitting on the crease above her chin. Her yellow teeth and bloodied gums were visible at all times. Her loose skin continued to sag towards the floor, tearing as it stretched. There were cuts on her abdomen, upper arms, and thighs and shins. Thick, yellow blisters surrounded the gashes.

She emitted a foul odor, like a corpse burning in a trench during a war. Her deterioration was accelerating despite her efforts to stop it. She wasn't dead, but she appeared to be rotting.

Ding!

The elevator arrived at the eighth floor.

"Apartment D, right?" Charlotte asked.

"Yeah, yeah..."

They hobbled down the hall, moving past two parallel doors. A cursive 'A' was painted over the door to the right and a cursive 'B' over the one to the left. Only the sounds of Charlotte's sneakers thudding and Cindy's sandals slapping the floor echoed through the corridors. The residents didn't hear them, though. They were protected from the outside world by sturdy doors, thick walls, and powerful sleeping pills.

They stopped in front of the second door to the left —the one with a cursive 'D' painted over it. She pressed the doorbell three times in rapid succession, then knocked on the door five times. She waited five seconds, then banged on the door five more times. She would have knocked more, but she heard the door's locks clicking and clacking.

As the door swung open, Deki said, "Cindy, you have to keep it down or..."

His voice petered off as he got a better look at his customer. He could only see the bottom half of her face, her hands, and legs—and that was enough to shock him. He opened his mouth to speak, but nothing came out.

Cindy scowled at him, revealing the rest of her teeth as her upper lip curled back. She was offended by his appearance. She had to suffer just to *try* to reach her image of perfection while Deki seemed to shine with effortless grace even at the dead of night. He wore a white tank top, black mesh shorts, and house slippers. His hair was messy but stylish, and his stubble was neatly trimmed. He hadn't changed much since the last time they met.

"I hope you don't mind if I eat all of your food," Cindy said. "I ran out on the way here and I'm starving."

She swiped at the bloody teardrops rolling down her cheeks with the back of her sleeves as she pushed past Deki. Deki stepped aside and watched her, incapable of chasing after her. Charlotte stayed in the hallway, waiting awkwardly for an invitation into the elegant penthouse.

Deki and Charlotte sat across from each other on separate recliners. The elegant coffee table between them had sturdy brass legs and a crystal glass top. There was a three-seat sofa to their left and an entertainment center with a large flat-screen television to their right. Thick curtains covered the floor-to-ceiling windows behind the entertainment center. Meanwhile, the parallel wall beyond the sofa looked like it was one big bookcase, shelves filled with novels, biographies, self-help books, and encyclopedias.

Paintings and family photographs hung on the

clean red walls. Under the seats and coffee table, there was an antique Sarouk Persian rug.

Is this what every drug dealer's home looks like? Charlotte thought. *Or only the ones in 'pharmaceuticals' and cartels?*

She could see into the kitchen through the archway in front of her. Cindy stood in front of a large refrigerator, rummaging for food. She left a trail of blood behind her. Her munching, slurping, and gulping echoed through the apartment. She devoured his vegetables and fruit and guzzled his fresh juice and milk. She swallowed raw eggs and let the broken eggshells fall to her feet. There was meat in the freezer, but it wasn't cooked. She had an urge to eat it raw, too, but she resisted.

Charlotte turned her attention to Deki, who was also looking over his shoulder at the kitchen archway. He was unnerved by her feral behavior.

"We obviously need your help," Charlotte said. "I plan on taking Cindy to the hospital no matter what, but she *really* wanted to come here first. She thinks you have the answer to her... 'problem.' I guess I get where she's coming from since you sold that *poison* to her. So, tell me: What did you put in those goddamn capsules?"

Deki kept staring at Cindy, as if in a hypnotic state. His fear was obvious thanks to his stiffness and the sweat on his forehead.

"Answer me," Charlotte said.

Keeping his eyes on Cindy, Deki said, "It's, um... It's complicated. I don't really know how to explain it."

"I don't need you to get scientific right now. I only need enough information to help Cindy. Something I can tell the doctors when we get to the hospital. Give us an idea of what we're working with so we know where to go. Okay?"

Deki sighed as he wrenched his gaze away from Cindy. Elbows on his knees and hands clasped, he looked down at the coffee table and said, "The capsule is a blend of... flesh- and fat-eating bacteria. E. coli, A. muciniphila, clostridium. There's more in there and it's a lot more complicated than that, but you get the idea. It's *bacteria*. It's an infection, obviously, but it doesn't spread. It's not like an STD or anything like that. And it's not supposed to be fatal. Even if you ignore the instructions and starve yourself, one or two capsules won't make you drop dead."

"It sounds like you're selling diseases to help people with diseases. That's horrible... But wait. If it's not supposed to be fatal, then what's happening to Cindy?"

"What we're seeing here is a... an overdose, I suppose. These capsules work well—*very well*. That's why she should have been eating to balance everything out. I told her this very clearly from the beginning. There might have been some side effects regardless, but if she followed my instructions, *this* wouldn't have happened. To be completely honest with you, whatever is happening to her right now, I've never seen anything like it before."

"I don't care if you've seen it before or not," Cindy said from the kitchen archway.

Deki and Charlotte glanced over at her. The sick woman leaned against the archway. She had a brick of cheese in her hand. There was more cheese in her mouth. She chewed it with her mouth open. Orange juice blended with the blood on her chin and neck. There wasn't much food left in the refrigerator.

Cindy wagged the block of cheese at Deki and said, "I want... an antidote. You hardly have any food in here. I mean, you... you live in a damn *penthouse*, but you don't have any food. What kind of person are you? Hmm? Don't you have a maid to go out and buy some groceries for you? Or a personal chef that can cook something up for you whenever you're hungry? Don't you... N–Never mind. Forget it. Just give me the antidote so I can leave this terrible place."

Deki said, "Cindy, there's... Shit, there is no antidote. I don't think I've ever even heard of an antidote in my line of work. I never really needed one. My clients have always followed my instructions."

"Give me an antidote," Cindy said sternly.

"I can't give you something that doesn't exist. What do you want me to do?"

Cindy snarled as she limped into the living room. She glared at Deki, her red eyes flaring with rage. Deki shrank in his seat and leaned away from her.

As she reached the sitting area, Cindy said, "You're going to fix this. You're going to save my life or... or else. If I run out of food around here, if I even *think* I'm going to die, I don't know what I'll do but it won't be pretty. You can't push a girl like me into a corner without expecting me to *bite* back. Get the antidote. *Now*."

Deki saw a beast in Cindy's eyes. He glanced over at Charlotte, hoping she would intervene. To his dismay, she was scared stiff, too.

"O–Okay," Deki croaked out. "I'll tell you what I can do for you. I'll, um... I'll call my supplier. They're my, uh... my business partners. I'll let them know about this situation and we'll see what happens. I don't want to promise you anything. I think that'll just make things worse between us, you know? I can't lie to you, this isn't looking good. So, until I can get ahold of my partners, you should eat whatever you can find in the kitchen. You might have to ask my neighbors for some food, too."

"You're asking me to beg for food?"

"I didn't say anything about begging."

"I've never asked my neighbors for a cup of sugar. You think I'm going to walk around the fucking Mosaic and beg your rich, snobby neighbors for food?"

"I think you're taking what I said the wrong–"

"Call your fucking suppliers and get me the damn antidote!" Cindy shouted. "Stop fucking with me, Deki! I'm... I'm rotting! I'm melting! Can't you see that?! You'll be responsible if I die! I'll make sure everyone knows about... about *this!*"

She lifted her shirt up to her collarbone, exposing her sagging stomach and wilting breasts. Her breasts had drifted away from each other, hanging close to her false ribs. Her nipples were inverted, pushed into her soft, wrinkled breasts. She pinched her right nipple and, with a gentle tug, she peeled it off like a sticker. It spiraled to the floor. Blood spilled out of her breast in a steady stream for five seconds, then slowed to a trickle. Most of the blood hit the marble floor and splashed on the rug, but some of it ran down her abdomen.

Yet, the woman's bloody face remained still. She didn't feel any physical pain from the self-mutilation.

"Help me," she said.

Charlotte and Deki stared at her in horror. Although they wanted to look away, shock paralyzed them for a moment. Charlotte gasped and turned away first—disgusted, horrified, depressed. She couldn't stand to see Cindy's deteriorating condition. She loved her too much to watch her die. Deki put his hand over his mouth and nodded rapidly, as if to say: *Yes, yes, I'll do whatever you say*. He felt his dinner climbing up to his throat, close to bursting out in the form of projectile vomit.

"I–I–I'll get right on it," he stammered from behind his hand. "Okay? I'll call my partners and I'll get everything I can from them now. I–I'm they're cash cow, you know? I can get ahold of them. You two... You just stay here and eat. Go in my kitchen and cook whatever you find. Um... Uh... When was the last time you took a capsule, Cindy? Think about it and be *completely* honest. No more lies. Did you take any today?"

"I haven't taken one in a few days. I'm clean, I swear."

Looking at the bookcases to avoid Cindy, Charlotte asked, "If she eats as much as possible, can she really fight this thing? Will she outlive the bacteria or whatever is in her?"

Deki stood from his seat and said, "She'll buy time. That's all I know for now. I'm going to make some calls." As he walked away, he said, "Eat, Cindy."

Cindy watched him hustle down a hallway behind Charlotte. She glanced back at the kitchen, then down at herself. She narrowed her eyes upon spotting her severed nipple on the floor. *Eat it*, a faint voice said from the back of her head. She started salivating at the thought of gobbling up her own nipple.

"Do you need a Band-Aid or something?" Charlotte asked, snapping her out of her trance.

"No. No, I'm fine," Cindy replied.

"Well, I'll, um... I'll get one for you later. I'll cook something for you now. Okay?"

"Yeah... thanks."

Cindy kept staring back at the nipple as Charlotte led her to the kitchen. Her cannibalistic urges grew stronger. She remembered eating her fingertip in her apartment.

It wasn't so bad, she told herself.

16

BY ANY MEANS NECESSARY

IN THE LIVING ROOM, CINDY SAT ON THE SOFA AND chewed on a peanut butter protein bar. Eight crumpled wrappers were piled up on the cushion next to her. She was about halfway through her ninth bar. They had discovered the box of snacks in one of Deki's cupboards. She could hear Charlotte cooking in the kitchen—pans *sizzling*, water *sloshing*, plates *clacking*.

Cindy stared at her reflection on the coffee table and thought about her bizarre situation. She was convinced that she was going to die soon, reduced to a heap of human slush. Although she had suicidal thoughts, she was still afraid of death. She wasn't ready to die. Survival was part of human nature, and she was willing to do *anything* to survive.

Fight, she told herself. *Do something.*

Charlotte walked into the living room. She placed a white ceramic plate on the table in front of Cindy.

There was a mound of white rice drizzled with soy sauce, chicken breasts, and boiled vegetables on it.

She handed Cindy a fork and said, "Eat up. I'll see what else I can cook up for you."

Cindy took another bite of the protein bar while staring down at the table. She looked distracted, completely unaware of Charlotte's presence or the plate in front of her.

Charlotte snapped her fingers at her and said, "Hey, Cin. Are you listening to me? What's wrong with you?"

Cindy stopped chewing. Then she stopped moving entirely for five seconds before swallowing the food in her mouth.

She looked up at Charlotte, took the fork from her hand, and said, "Thank you."

"Are you okay?"

Cindy bent over and shoved a forkful of rice into her mouth. While chewing the rice, she scooped up a piece of chicken with her other hand and slid it past her teeth. She ate as quickly as possible, as if she were taking part in a competitive eating contest. Fearing she was going to choke, Charlotte ran to the kitchen to get a cup of water. By the time she returned, Cindy had already cleaned her plate.

Chewing on the vegetables, Cindy said, "I need... more. This isn't... enough. I need something... *something* bigger."

Charlotte set the cup down next to the plate and

said, "I'll see what else I can cook up. There's still some more rice in the kitchen."

"I need more... I need more..."

"I'll get you more. Just hang in there, okay? I'll be right back."

As Charlotte hurried into the kitchen, Cindy muttered, "I don't need friends. No, I need food. I need *real* food, damn it. I'll... I'll die if I don't save myself. Yeah, *I* have to do something. *Me*, not them. They... They don't care about me. They never did. They probably want me to die so they can get rid of me. But I can't die. Not like this."

She glanced around the lavish apartment, eyes welling with bloody tears. She considered knocking on the neighbors' doors and asking for food. The idea sounded ridiculous, though. She couldn't imagine one of Deki's yuppie neighbors showing sympathy for a woman with her bloodied, grotesque appearance. She assumed the neighbors would call the Centers for Disease Control and Prevention as soon as they saw her instead of offering a helping hand.

She whispered, "I'm hideous. I'm a freak, a–a... a monster. I can't be seen like this, but I have to do something. What do I do? What do I do?"

She stared at the wall to her left while absently scraping her plate with the fork. It made short but sharp screeching sounds each time. Her imagination ran wild. She wondered about the CDC's response to her bizarre condition. *A group of people in hazmat suits will raid the apartment and trap me in here like an animal,* she thought. *It would be all over the news, my name and picture broadcast all around the world.*

She shook her head, refusing to accept the possibility. She looked over at the corridor to her right. She could see Deki pacing between two rooms at the end of the hall. He held a cell phone up to his ear. His hushed voice barely reached the living room. She couldn't make out a word, but she could tell he was distraught by his fidgeting and frowning. Cindy's appearance sickened him and her threats frightened him.

"What the hell is taking you so long, Deki?" Cindy whispered. "What are you planning?"

She leaned and scooted a little more to her right. Deki's voice grew louder, tight with concern. His conversation with his business partner was snowballing into an argument.

"I don't know," Deki was saying. "She's sick. She's dying, man."

There was a pause. He kept pacing between the rooms. He started biting on his thumb's fingernail and nodding.

He said, "She won't last long. Send someone to clean..." His voice trailed off as he walked into a room. As he emerged in the hallway again, he said, "And do it before the cops show up. Her mess is..."

And once more, his voice faded away as he walked into another room. *He's going to let me die,* Cindy thought, her teeth chattering. *Then he's going to throw me away like garbage*. She leaned back in her seat and stared at the fork in her hand. In the penthouse, in the world of the rich and heartless, she was expendable. She wasn't even good enough for a housekeeper. Her mess was reserved for a crime scene cleaner. Her life was insignificant.

She looked back at the hall and whispered, "You think you can get rid of me just like that? You think you can just clean me up like a spilled drink? You must be crazy, Deki. I won't let you do this to me. I'm done being walked all over, done being treated like trash, done with you people, done... done with this lie of a life."

———

Charlotte walked into the living room. She approached the sofa and peeked down the hall, curious and hopeful. She hadn't heard anything from Deki since he ran off to make his phone call. She sat next to Cindy and carefully put her arm around her.

She said, "I have some mac and cheese in the oven. It should be finished in a few minutes. I remember you used to love it when we were in high school. Freshman year, remember? You'd come over to my house and my mom would always invite you to stay for dinner. And you'd *only* stay if she was making mac and cheese." The smile on Charlotte's face came and went in a matter of seconds. She said, "It feels like such a long time ago, doesn't it? It's almost like a dream. Or maybe this just feels like a nightmare right now, huh? I just wish..."

Cindy's attention wandered to the hallway. Charlotte's voice became a muffled hum in her head. She could only think about the future. The past was meaningless if she wasn't around to remember it. Heartwarming memories couldn't save her. Food was her only option. She turned her head to look at Charlotte. She watched as her friend's plump lips flapped with each word out of her mouth. She leered at her curvy torso, then at her legs. Her admiration for her turned into an *appetite* for her. She brought her gaze back up until she was gazing into her glimmering eyes.

Despite all of the death and carnage, Charlotte's eyes glowed with hope. A kind soul was operating her beautiful figure. She was perfect, inside and out.

"I'm so sorry," Cindy said, a bloody tear dribbling down her cheek.

"You don't have anything to be sorry for," Charlotte said. "I should be the one–"

"I'm sorry for what I'm going to do to you."

"Huh? Wha–What are you–"

Cindy lunged at Charlotte and bit the center of her neck. Her teeth pierced the muscles around her thyroid cartilage. Blood jetted from Charlotte's neck. It splashed on the sofa and ran down to her collarbones. Face crumpled up in pain, Charlotte leaned over the armrest next to her and bellowed a bloodcurdling scream. She grasped Cindy's shoulders and pushed her, but that only worsened the wound on her neck and increased the pain.

Cindy bit down harder—so hard that only her gums were visible. Her predatory instincts took over, forcing her to shake her head ferociously, like a wolf trying to snap its prey's spine. Charlotte's muscles and skin *crinkled* and *crunched*. Her shriek, only a few seconds long, was cut short, replaced by groaning and gurgling sounds. Her larynx was ruptured and blood filled her windpipe. The noise from her struggle echoed through the halls outside of the penthouse, dying off at the elevator bank.

Cindy yanked her head back, tearing a big nugget of flesh off Charlotte's neck. She slurped and chewed and gulped. Charlotte rolled off the sofa and put both of her hands over the bloody crater on her neck, as if she were strangling herself. Her windpipe was still intact, but she had trouble breathing on account of her severed larynx and all of the blood she was gargling. On her knees and elbows, she wormed her way around the sofa.

The sudden attack scrambled her thoughts. Although the front door was closer, she crawled towards the hallway to find Deki, believing only he could save her. She moved at a snail's pace, leaving a trail of blood behind her. By the time she reached the hallway, Cindy was finished eating her flesh. The act of cannibalism reinvigorated her. A fresh coat of blood covered her mouth, chin, and neck.

Following the trail of blood, she said, "I'm sorry, Char, but it's over. You're already dead. You're only prolonging your suffering. Let me help you like you helped me. Let me put you out of your misery."

Charlotte kept crawling. In the hallway, yellow light came out of the last room to the right. She could see Deki's shadow. He was moving around restlessly. Charlotte felt herself fading, getting weaker and weaker with each drop of blood leaking out of her neck. So, she dragged herself into the first room to her left. It was a spacious bathroom.

A dead end.

Cindy continued following her at a leisurely pace, unhurried and unconcerned. She said, "That was your plan, wasn't it? You were sick and tired of me—tired of my depression, my complaining, my fatness—so you wanted to put me out of my misery. Wanted to drop me off at a hospital and let me die there or watch me melt here and flush me down a toilet. Then what were you going to do? Fuck Deki?"

She stopped in the doorway just as Charlotte kicked the door. She used her elbow to push it open and stop it from slamming up against her face.

She said, "I didn't want it to end like this. I *loved* you, Charlotte. But I knew, deep down, you always hated me."

Charlotte reached the end of the bathroom. There

was a round bathtub in front of her. Beyond the bathtub, there was a floor-to-ceiling window overlooking the city. Cindy grabbed Charlotte's head from behind, then rammed it against the tub. Charlotte's right temple tore open. Her grip on her neck weakened, allowing the blood cupped in her hands to spill onto the tile floor. Although dazed by the blow, she remained conscious, gasping for air.

Cindy rolled her onto her side and mounted her waist. She chomped at Charlotte's face. She was slim, so there wasn't much loose skin for her teeth to grip. She tore off the tail of her left eyebrow with the first bite. With the second, she ripped off a wedge of skin from her cheekbone. Then her teeth sliced the corner of her eye and grazed her eyeball with the third and fourth chomps. Blood filled her left eye socket first, then ran down over the bridge of her nose and filled the other before connecting to the gash on her temple.

Charlotte blindly elbowed Cindy's face, ripping her lower lip off. Cindy felt a mere pinch of pain. The fact that she had lost her lip bothered her more than the pain.

"You bitch," she hissed. "Look at what you did to me! Look at what you're making me do!"

She grabbed a fistful of Charlotte's hair and dragged her to the toilet next to a counter. She kicked the seat up, then thrust Charlotte's head into the bowl. While doing so, Charlotte's neck hit the rim. The wide hole on her neck stretched open. Blood gushed out of her mouth and throat. It billowed through the sloshing water, turning it all red in an instant.

Charlotte swung her submerged head around, but she couldn't break free. The bloody water bubbled around her head. It entered her body through her mouth and the hole in her neck, filling her lungs like water balloons. Her feet slid on the puddle of blood behind her while her hands slipped off the bowl repeatedly. She stopped flailing after twenty seconds.

Despite the lack of resistance, Cindy kept pushing her head down for another minute. She glared at her friend while bloody teardrops fell from her eyes and landed on the back of Charlotte's head. She felt a combination of anger and sadness, as if she were killing her mortal enemy and best friend at the same time.

She deserves it, the little voice in Cindy's head whispered.

Cindy pulled her friend's head out of the bowl and studied her pale face. Although she continued to twitch, Charlotte had passed away from the loss of blood, shock, and suffocation.

Cindy kissed her forehead, then said, "I loved you."

She lay Charlotte's lifeless body down next to the toilet, like a drunk at a house party. She stood up, feeling stronger than ever. Tasting the blood in her mouth, she connected the burst of strength to the consumption of Charlotte's neck. She ran her eyes over her friend's corpse. Her gaze settled on her breasts. She thought about cutting them off and baking them in the oven.

Then she heard footsteps in the hallway.

Deki, she thought.

She stepped out of the bathroom and looked to her right. She found Deki standing in the middle of the hallway. He had been taking two steps forward and one step back, inching his way to the exit. He was rigid now, ashen-faced with fear. He held his cell phone in his right hand with his shaky thumb over the green CALL prompt. He had dialed 911, but he hadn't called yet.

"Hello, doctor," Cindy said, monotone.

Deki stuttered, "Wha–What did you do?"

"I'm doing what you told me to do. Eat or be eaten."

"N–No, you... Oh God, what the hell did you do?!"

"It's like I told Charlotte. I'm not a piece of trash you can just throw away. I'm not a mess you can mop up or flush down the toilet."

"What are you–"

"I will *not* become a freak of nature in a cage, paraded around for the world to see. I'm *not* dying here. And I'm not done with you, Dr. Deki."

Deki staggered back as Cindy took a step towards him. Without thinking, he opened the door to his right, entered the room, then slammed the door behind him. He moved so quickly that even he was impressed by his speed. He was in a small storage closet. Coats hung from a rod to his left. Cleaning supplies filled the shelves to his right. There was a vacuum cleaner in front of him. He reached for the doorknob and groped about for a lock. It took him a second to realize the door didn't have a lock and he had inadvertently cornered himself.

He heard Cindy's footsteps as she closed in on the closet. He grabbed the doorknob and leaned against the door, using his weight to anchor it down, then he called 911.

———

"Open up," Cindy said as she leaned against the closet door. "C'mon, don't be like this. I'm here for my checkup, hon."

Holding his cell phone up to his ear, Deki yelled, "Stay back!"

"911, what is your emergency?" a female operator answered his call.

Deki said, "A–A woman broke into my home! I think she killed someone!" Believing a lie would expedite the police response, he yelled, "I think she's armed and drugged out of her mind! She had a–a knife! And she's biting people over here!"

The operator asked, "Where are you now, sir?"

"The Mosaic Apartments! Apartment 8D! Eight-D, okay?!"

"I understand, sir. Are you in a safe place?"

Cindy leaned against the door and said, "The

police can't save you. When I'm done with you, there won't be anything left to save."

She turned the knob and rammed the door with her shoulder. It popped open an inch. Deki pushed it closed again.

"No!" Deki cried. "I–I'm in the closet! She's trying to break the door down!"

"I'm sending a unit now," the operator said. "Sir, can you barricade the door?"

"No, no. I–I can't. There's no lock on this fucking thing!"

"I need you to–"

The phone slid out of Deki's hand as Cindy tackled the door. It opened two inches. Deki leaned on his side of the door while Cindy leaned against hers. Despite losing so much weight with the miracle capsules, Cindy was still heavier than the fake doctor. She planted her foot in the doorway, using the loose skin drooping around her ankles like a rubber doorstop wedge. She hit the door with her shoulder again. It opened enough for her to slip her arm through the gap.

Palms planted on the door, pushing with all of his might, Deki looked down at his phone and shouted, "Hurry up! She's going to kill me! Send someone! Anyone! Please!"

The door flew open. Deki crashed into the wall next to the vacuum cleaner. He swung his head in every direction in search of a weapon. The vacuum cleaner caught his eye. It was the largest object in the closet, but it was also too light to do any damage. He stopped searching upon hearing Cindy's snicker. He saw her standing in the doorway with a wry smile on her face.

She asked, "You wanna know something silly?"

"Stay away from me, you psycho!"

"When I first met you, I actually believed you were one of the good ones. I fantasized about dating you. I imagined us as the perfect couple. I just needed to lose that weight and everything would have been... magical. Happily ever after, y'know?"

Keeping his eyes on Cindy, Deki tilted his head to the side and shouted, "Help! Help me!"

"I let my guard down and trusted you, and you betrayed me. That was my fault. You were planning on letting me die and throwing me out with the garbage. But you know what were your mistakes? You talk too loud and–"

"Help me, goddammit!"

"–you should have never let me into your home in the first place. I won't let you get away from me. If I die, *you die.*"

Cindy rushed into the closet, arms outstretched in front of her. Deki was appalled by her appearance—so disgusted that he didn't want to lay a finger on her—but he knew he had to defend himself. He struck her jaw with a swift jab, causing her to lurch to her right and crash into the shelves. He seized the opportunity and hit her again, unleashing a barrage of punches—left, right, left, right, *left, right*. Most of the jabs landed on the back of her head with hollow thuds.

Yet, Cindy stayed on her feet. The punches hurt Deki's fists more than they hurt her skull. She started snickering, amused by the attack.

Frustrated by her laughter, Deki screamed and hit her with a hook. The haymaker landed directly on her nose. Cindy stumbled back and grabbed onto the coats to stop herself from falling. Her nose was crushed like a piece of gum on a sidewalk. Blood leaked out of her nostrils, which were now flattened into slits. It blended with the blood in her mouth—hers and Charlotte's.

Out of breath, Deki said, "Why won't you..."

He stopped speaking as she lifted her right arm. She held a green spray bottle in her hand. The label on the side read: *CLOROX*. She sprayed the bleach in his face—twice for good measure. Deki was instantly blinded by the liquid. Howling, he put his hands over his face and teetered back. His eyes stung and reddened. It got in his mouth, too, making his taste buds buzz and his lips quiver.

Cindy dropped the bottle and pounced on him. She pushed him up against the wall and chomped at his shoulder, sinking her teeth into his upper trapezius muscle. She moaned as she gnawed on it. Blood flowed down his arm and chest. Due to the unbearable pain in his eyes, he couldn't muster the strength to push her off.

Cindy pulled her head back, stretching his muscle away from his body until she ripped a chunk of it off. One of his tank top's straps was torn with it. She let the severed muscle fall to the floor between them, then she bit his ear. Her teeth pierced the bottom half of it. She felt his earlobe on her tongue. She jerked her head to the side and tore it in half.

She spit the amputated ear at his face and giggled. She chomped at his ear again, hoping to sever the rest of it, but Deki leaned away from her. Back against the wall, he slid to his right and hid his head behind the hanging coats. Sobbing, he put his elbow against her chest to keep her at bay. During the struggle, the vacuum cleaner tipped over and hit the wall next to the shelves.

"S–Stop!" Deki cried. "Don't! Please don't!"

Since she couldn't reach his ear, Cindy bit the side of his neck. Her teeth surrounded his jugular. She felt the thick vein snaking around in her mouth. She pulled her head back in an attempt to rip his throat out, but her grip slackened as Deki thrust his elbow at her neck. She let him go and gagged. Blood sprayed out of the holes on the man's neck, splattering on the wall and floor.

Cindy jumped forward and bit his neck again. She clamped her teeth around his Adam's apple. She shook her head to loosen his flesh. She slurped up his blood, then gulped it down—one mouthful after another. Although weakened by the loss of blood,

Deki prodded Cindy's throat with his elbow a second time.

He slid down to the floor with his hand wrapped around his neck. Cindy tottered back and coughed up a storm of blood.

"I... trusted... you," she said, her voice low and harsh.

"Plee–Please," Deki squeaked out. "I don't... don't want to... die."

Cindy said, "Yeah? Too bad. It's time... for you to learn... what I learned a long time ago." She straddled his lap and said, "Life. Isn't. Fair."

She grabbed the sides of his head and dug her thumbs into his eye sockets. Deki shrieked and squirmed under her. The back of his head, his shoulders, and his elbows banged against the wall behind him. The pain spreading across his face and pulsing through his brain was tremendous. Cindy wiggled her thumbs—which were more bone than flesh now—around in his eye sockets, as if she were moving the joysticks of a game controller. She tried to hook her thumbs around his eyes to pull them out, but she couldn't jam them in.

Deki's eyes were bloodshot and bleeding, irritated and sliced. The bloody tears cascaded across his cheeks and dripped from his jaw. His twitching eyelids turned dark red. Cindy slid her thumb between his left eyeball and nose, causing the eye to bulge out a little. She tugged on it by curling her thumb, but it wouldn't budge. Over Deki's gasping and groaning, she could hear the muscles attached to his eyeball *crackling* under the strain. She screamed and smashed the back of Deki's head against the wall three times. His unconscious body was slumped to his left.

Cindy searched for a tool to help her remove his eye. She thought about using one of the clothes hangers. As she turned to check the shelves, the vacuum cleaner caught her attention. Grinning, she plugged it into a socket next to the shelves, then grabbed its hose. She pressed the big, circular nozzle against Deki's left eye.

"The perfect fit," she said.

She pressed the power switch on the vacuum cleaner. Deki's eye was pulled deeper into the nozzle, awakening him with a fresh bolt of pain. His screaming was as loud as the vacuum's roaring. Meanwhile, the nozzle made a *hissing* sound as his eye clogged it. Cindy cackled maniacally. From her eyebrows to her jaw, her smiling face was drenched in blood. Only her forehead remained clean.

A loud *crunch* came from Deki's skull. At the same moment, Deki blacked out. The muscles around his eye had torn. His eyeball was sucked out of his skull and into the nozzle. It only moved an inch before it got jammed in there and the vacuum cleaner automatically turned off on its own. Only the severed optic nerve hung out from the nozzle like a noodle.

"You should have kept your eyes to yourself," Cindy

said as she gazed into his hollowed eye socket. "Should have never looked at me at that gym."

Still unconscious, Deki fell to his side. Cindy grabbed the back of his head in one hand and his face with the other. She lifted his head, then thrust it down on the hard floor. The *thud* echoed through the apartment. She picked his head up, then slammed it on the floor again and again—and again. She smashed his head on the floor *seven* times. After the seventh blow, blood flowed out of Deki's ear canal in a steady stream. Although he had stopped breathing, his body kept twitching and faint groaning sounds came out of his mouth.

———

Cindy rolled Deki onto his back. She picked his head up and sucked the blood out of his eye socket, as if she were sipping hot soup from a bowl. Thick and dark, the blood was mixed with the vitreous fluid from his eye. She swished it around in her mouth, savoring its metallic tang, then swallowed it all with one loud gulp.

She *ahhed* in delight, as if she had just taken a swig of Coca-Cola on a hot summer day. She licked the blood off his face. It tasted saltier due to tears on his cheeks.

Staring at his face, she said, "Oh, don't give me that look. You know you deserved this. You should have been there for me. I mean, what kind of doctor abandons his patients? Hmm? Don't blame me for this, asshole. This is your fault. All of this is *your* fault."

She nodded at him, then she huffed and shook her head, as if he had answered her with an absurd reply. She took the piece of trapezius muscle off the floor and started to nibble away at it.

Between bites, she said, "Fuck you, Deki... *Fuck you*. I knew you were an asshole... from the first moment I saw you. I know, *I'm* stupid for trusting you, but... but *you're* stupid and *dead* for letting me into your home. Yeah, you think about that while you rot in hell, motherfucker."

She shoved the rest of the muscle into her mouth and she struggled to her feet. As she walked towards the door, she noticed Deki's phone on the floor. The call had disconnected during the brawl.

She glanced back at Deki and said, "I better get going before the cops show up, huh? You guys tasted pretty good, but I'm not in the mood for bacon."

Cindy picked up the cell phone, turned it off, then put it in her pocket. She made her way to the bathroom.

She nodded at Charlotte's corpse and asked, "How's it going?"

Her friend's death didn't bother her. There wasn't a shred of guilt or shame in her body. She went to the sink and washed her hands and face. She used the hottest water possible. Steam rose from the sink and fogged up the mirror in front of her. Yet, she didn't feel any pain from the scalding water.

"I'm feeling better already," she said. She looked at Charlotte and said, "I feel stronger than ever. And... it's all because of you, isn't it?"

Cindy realized that the human flesh had revitalized her. Since devouring her friend and dealer, she was able to walk without a limp and talk without a frog in her throat. She didn't need anyone to carry her or drive her around. She wasn't cured—she could still *feel* the bacteria eating her from within—but her hope was rekindled.

She stood over Charlotte's body, leering at her like a pervert at a gym. She couldn't help but smirk as she stared into her vacant eyes. She finally had something Charlotte didn't have: *Life*. She could continue on her pursuit of happiness, bulldozing through anyone in her path. On the other hand, Charlotte's story ended in a stranger's penthouse while attempting to help a woman who secretly despised her.

Cindy said, "Thank you for everything, hon. I guess I'll see you in another life." She kissed her passionately, gently biting and pulling on her lower lip, then said, "I thought about doing that before. It wasn't as exciting as I thought it would be. Too bad."

Cindy laughed as she walked out of the bathroom. She strutted over to the kitchen, swinging her hips while humming a jolly tune. She opened the oven and tried to take a big whiff. Due to her busted nose, she couldn't smell a thing. She grabbed the round baking dish from the oven and a fork from the counter. The thinning skin on her fingers peeled, but she didn't feel the heat from the dish on her hands. She was immune to pain. She sat down and scarfed down the macaroni and cheese in under a minute.

Chewing the last mouthful, she walked back into the living room and hollered, "It's a little too crispy, but I can't complain. You're a great cook. Just like your mom, Char. Maybe even better." As she walked to the front door, she shouted, "Thanks again! I'll see you around!"

Cindy walked out of the apartment and shut the door behind her. Moving with confidence, she went to the elevator bank down the hall and called an elevator. She escaped the crime scene with only one thing on her mind: *Food*. She knew her burst of energy wasn't going to last forever and she was going to have to eat a lot more if she wanted to survive. She wasn't concerned, though. Food was everywhere.

People were everywhere.

17

APEX PREDATOR

THE WAIL OF POLICE SIRENS ECHOED THROUGH THE CITY, quickly growing louder as patrol cars raced to the crime scene at the Mosaic Apartments. Cars cluttered the busiest intersections, drivers dozing in and out of consciousness while waiting for the traffic lights to change. Some teenagers rode their bicycles on the sidewalks and homeless people slept at bus stops and in alleyways. The cold wind blew trash—food wrappers, plastic bags, crushed cans, torn flyers—through the streets.

No one paid any attention to Cindy as she roamed the affluent neighborhood. The residents and drivers could see her walking on the sidewalk, but her sagging skin was hidden by the darkness of the night. Her clothing piqued their curiosity—it looked like she was only wearing a large coat from afar—but it didn't concern them enough to force them to intervene. As long as she stayed away from their property, the rich residents didn't care about her.

Cindy had cleaned herself in Deki's bathroom, but water couldn't repair her busted nose or reattach her lower lip. Although she was no longer ashamed of her appearance, she hid her face under the hood of her coat to keep the element of surprise. Gusts of wind hit her bare legs, but like the scalding water, she didn't notice the chilly weather. She could still taste the macaroni and cheese as well as the blood in her mouth. Her stomach growled for more.

"What's next on the menu?" she whispered.

She looked up at the tall luxury apartment buildings around her, then she inspected the entrances. The buildings were like resorts with front desk receptionists, concierges, and 24-hour security. Depending on the staff, some of the buildings were easier to infiltrate than others. Regardless, the apartment buildings offered too many options—too many variables. It was hard for her to pick the perfect target when she couldn't scope out the homes.

She figured she was better off rummaging through the houses a few blocks away. She turned and hurried down a dark alley. The emergency sirens softened as she put some distance between herself and the Mosaic Apartments. She assumed the police had arrived at the crime scene. She wondered how long it would take them to identify her and set up a manhunt. She sped up her pace to a brisk walk, hoping to escape the police and ready to attack the unsuspecting homeowners.

Halfway down the alley, her temples began to throb. Pain zapped through her head, as if a bullet were ricocheting in her skull. She lost her balance and crashed into the dumpster next to her. She fell to a knee with her shoulder against the dumpster.

"I need... to eat," she said in a pained voice, rubbing her temples and holding her breath. "It... can't... wait."

She got up to her feet and pushed the dumpster lid skyward. She examined the pit of rotting garbage. She couldn't smell the trash due to her obliterated nose. The awful stench wafted out of the dumpster, growing stronger in the alley and rising to the apartments above. Some residents slammed their windows shut upon catching a whiff of it. Flies buzzed around her, like military planes trying to shoot King Kong off the Empire State Building.

The dumpster was filled to the brim. Some of the plastic bags were torn open by a broken vase. There were crumpled food wrappers, cartons of milk, discarded pizza boxes and oyster pails, empty bottles and crushed cans, and used condoms and syringes in there. Most of it was inedible and all of it was unappetizing.

It didn't matter to Cindy, though. She dove in headfirst. She ripped a carton of milk open. It still had some chunky, rotten milk in it, so she slurped it up. It was more sour than sweet. She opened the pizza box and scraped the old, crusty cheese off it. It reeked and tasted like the sour milk. She snatched up the condom, which was tied up in a knot like a balloon.

The rubber had brown streaks and the tip was filled with yellowish semen. She stared at the semen for a few seconds. *It's gotta have some nutrients,* she thought. *And it can't be worse than rotten food.* She ripped it open with her teeth, then drank the semen. And to her utter surprise, it *was* worse than the rotten food and human flesh she had consumed.

Grimacing in disgust, she tossed the broken condom aside, then continued searching the dumpster. Her eyes widened upon spotting a furry leg sticking out from under a mountain of plastic bags. She pushed the bags aside, then cocked her head back.

A dead cat was buried under the trash. With stiff limbs and a flattened torso, it looked like its body had been steamrolled. Maggots wiggled around a large hole on its chest and gathered around its gaping mouth. The cat's black fur was matted with dried blood and mud.

She pulled the carcass out, then sat on the ground with her back to the dumpster. She placed the cat on her lap and swiped the maggots off it, as if she were brushing its fur with her fingers. With hesitation in her eyes, she glanced over at the torn condom next to her, then up at the apartment buildings around her. She thought about the murders and cannibalism at the Mosaic Apartments.

"I've already gone this far," she murmured. "I can't stop now."

She lifted the carcass up to her chest. She drew a deep breath, then another, and then she shut her eyes and chomped into the cat's torso. She snarled and shook her head, trying to tear a chunk off it. The sound of shredding flesh clashed with a rattling noise in the alley. A maggot wiggled into her mouth, but she ignored it. Survival was her only concern.

The rattling noise stopped.

Mouth full of cat flesh, fur, blood, and maggots, Cindy glanced over to her left. An elderly man stood just a few meters away from her. Greasy white hair stuck out from his threadbare beanie, and he had a bushy, grizzled beard. He was missing two of his upper incisor teeth. He wore layers of tattered coats and sweatpants. His boots were dirty and scuffed but sturdy.

He had been pushing a shopping cart around. There were some plastic bags filled with crushed cans, sheets of cardboard, a backpack, and a folded blanket in the cart.

Cindy could tell he was homeless. With her eyes stuck on the guy, she flung her head back and tore a small piece of flesh off the carcass.

Chewing the rotting meat, she said, "Keep walking, bud. This one's mine."

Goggle-eyed and mouth ajar, the homeless man stared at her in total disbelief. He walked around his shopping cart to get a better view of her, hoping his eyes were playing a trick on him. But his disbelief rapidly turned into horror and disgust. He had seen plenty of dead cats before—and the one in Cindy's hands was no prop. It was all real.

He checked both sides of the alley. He heard faint sirens, but he didn't see any people or cars. He looked back at Cindy. The horror on his face was gone. He was still disgusted by her actions, but he pitied her more than anything. He was a nice guy with bad luck, so he didn't see a cannibalistic killer sitting before him. He saw a hungry, desperate, sick woman.

He knelt in front of her and, in a gravelly but kind voice, he said, "My God, you must be starving. Put... Put that down, will ya? C'mon, tell me your name. What are you doing out here like this?"

Cindy picked a lock of fur from between her teeth with her fingernail, then spit it at the man's feet. He didn't flinch. It wasn't the first time someone spit at him and he was positive it wasn't going to be the last.

"What do you care?" Cindy asked.

The homeless man smiled thinly and said, "My name is Charles. Charles Hamilton. You can call me 'Charlie' if you'd like. It's friendlier, I think."

"That's great, Charlie, but you're not getting to the point. What the hell do you want from me? I told you already, this one's mine. As a matter of fact, this whole dumpster's mine. If you wanna go diving, go find your own dumpster."

"I don't want to steal your... 'food.' Listen, I've been around for a long time. Hell, I've been homeless for longer than I can remember. I've been in your shoes before. I know the lengths that people will go to for survival. I guess I just... I wanted to offer you a helping hand. That's all. You can think of it as my good deed of the day. It is a new day after all."

"You want to help me? *Why?*"

Charlie couldn't make out much of her disfigured face due to her hood, the darkness, and his own poor eyesight. He noticed the bloody smears on her chin and neck, though. He assumed the blood came from the carcass. And judging from her injuries and deranged behavior, he guessed she was on a drug binge.

Bath salts, he thought.

He said, "I used to be hooked on dope. Used to inject black tar heroin—the good dope, y'know?—a couple of times a week. I sold my body and soul for it. I ate, uh... Well, let's just say I often ate things that were much worse than a dead cat just to live a little bit longer. I got off it, though. It took a *long* time, but I did it. Been clean for years now. I found confidence in myself, I joined a support group, and I searched for *real* happiness and *real* purpose in my life. Now, I won't pressure you into anything, but I can help you escape your addiction if... if that's what you want. I can help you find the light. What do you say?"

Cindy stared at him with a deadpan expression.

The guy was sincere, but he was also confused. Watching Cindy, he saw a reflection of his past and he saw an opportunity to redeem himself. Cindy was a victim of drug abuse, but she didn't use any of the common street narcotics. She was nothing like Charlie.

She said, "I don't need to find 'the light.' Actually, I think I prefer the dark. You can help me out, though."

"How? I can't help you get more drugs and I don't have any money to give. I got some water and snacks in my bag, though. A lot better than... that 'meal' you got there."

"Food will do."

"Sure, sure. I been saving up a couple of chocolate bars," Charlie said. He chuckled, then said, "I've got a sweet tooth, y'know? Give me a sec. I'll get something for ya."

Charlie stood up and walked back to his shopping cart. While he looked through his backpack, Cindy dropped the carcass and pulled herself up to her feet.

Charlie said, "Now, these are a little old, but they should still be good. Do you like dark or–"

In one swift move, Cindy grabbed him from behind, jumped up, and bit the side of his neck. Charlie screamed and stumbled away from his shopping cart. He fell face-first on the pavement. His nose was broken, his remaining teeth were chipped, and his upper lip was split open vertically down the middle. Crumbs of brown enamel and drops of blood hit the ground under his face.

Meanwhile, Cindy had bitten him so hard that her teeth punctured his internal jugular vein. His blood filled her mouth faster than she could swallow it. Charlie writhed under her. The rapid loss of blood and the blow to the face left him stunned. He felt like the world was spinning around him—like he was free-falling from 20,000 feet in the air.

Unable to breathe with all of the blood in her mouth, Cindy released his neck. Two more spurts of blood gushed out of his severed jugular, then the bleeding slowed. Charlie clawed at the pavement and dragged himself out from under her, his brittle finger-nails snapping in the process. He crawled past the dumpster. He saw a car race down the street at the end of the alley.

"He... Help," he rasped. "Help... me."

Cindy grabbed his leg. She pushed his pant leg up and pulled his socks down, then she bit his heel. With a jerk of her head, she pulled him back an inch. She chewed and sucked on his heel, moaning in delight. On his elbows, Charlie tried to crawl forward again, but he only placed more pressure on his mutilated ankle.

After a minute, his Achilles tendon was severed. He felt the cord slither up his leg. He put his hand on his knee, rolled onto his side, and sobbed. He started convulsing. With a piece of his Achilles tendon in her mouth, Cindy crawled up to him. She chewed on it, savoring the tang of his blood. It was too durable for her to grind it down to a smaller piece, though.

She spit the mushy tendon at Charlie's face, then said, "Sorry, mister, but I don't need anyone's help anymore. I just need blood. Lots and lots of blood. You've got plenty of that, don't you?"

"Don't... I... only... want... wanted... to help... you."

"Believe me, you're helping me more than you can possibly imagine. You are my light, Charlie. And now I'm going to take your light and put it in me. You're going to help me live... forever."

She bit the side of his neck again. The *crunching* and *plopping* and *slurping* echoed through the alleyway. It reached the apartments above and the surrounding streets. Yet, the cars continued zooming past the alley and the residents continued ignoring the brutal attack. If it didn't involve them or their property, it wasn't important to them.

Cindy ripped Charlie's neck open. She spit a chunk of severed muscle at his face, then unleashed a loud, angry scream—*a battle cry*. Then, while catching her breath, she heard another window slam shut above them.

She giggled, then said, "They don't care about people like us. No one cares about the outcasts until we step out of the shadows. It's every man for himself in this world. That's life. But don't you worry about a thing. I'm going to step out of the shadows and I'm going to get revenge for the both of us."

Charlie's eyelids fluttered and his head swayed. Vision blurry and dark, he could barely see the outline of Cindy's body above him. Her voice was masked by the ringing and thumping in his ears. He started to hyperventilate as he reached for his mangled neck. He couldn't reach the wounds, though. Instead, his hands shook so badly that it looked like he was purposely pounding away at his chest.

Cindy watched the color fade from his face. His eyes appeared to change from blue to silver and his cheeks from white to gray. With one final exhale, the homeless man passed away.

She caressed his forehead and said, "Thank you for your sacrifice."

She leaned closer to Charlie's face and sucked the severed muscle into her mouth, causing her cheeks to inflate. Chewing on the muscle, she went over to the shopping cart and rifled through his belongings. In his backpack, she found an extra coat, a few pamphlets for a local substance abuse support group, and a neatly rolled newspaper. In the smaller pocket, she found five chocolate bars and an empty tin can. She took the chocolate and left the can. She didn't plan on begging for money anyway.

As she unwrapped one of the chocolate bars, she glanced down the alley and whispered, "It's not enough. I need more."

She looked at Charlie's corpse and considered eating more of him, but then she heard another emergency siren. Following her original plan, she hurried down the alley and headed towards the houses a few blocks away.

———

The human flesh had revitalized Cindy, but it didn't fix her squashed nose. So, she found herself wheezing while eating her last chocolate bar. Disoriented due to the lack of oxygen, she waddled down the sidewalk with her head spinning. She was wandering around a cozy middle-class neighborhood—the type with white picket fences and SUVs in the driveways. The streetlights weren't very bright, so she had trouble finding the perfect target.

Hidden by the darkness, the houses looked identical from the streets. All of them stood two stories tall with their front lawns kept trim and ample space in the backyards. She had over a hundred options in the neighborhood. To her dismay, many of them had home security signposts in their lawns. She couldn't tell which were real and which were fake. She didn't want to cause another scene. She felt the massacre at the Mosaic Apartments catching up to her.

"Oh, come on," Cindy muttered. "Not all of you can be fucking home security specialists. One of you must have left your door open. One of you..."

She stopped speaking upon hearing the purr of a car engine behind her. A beam of light dawned on the slab of sidewalk in front of her. She crouched behind a truck parked on the street, narrowly evading the oncoming vehicle's headlights. A white van cruised past her, rolling at around ten miles per hour. It stopped in the driveway five houses down.

Convenient, Cindy thought.

Knuckle-walking like a gorilla, she moved down the sidewalk while staying low. She stopped after passing three houses and peeked over a picket fence. She saw a man exit the white van through the driver's door. A woman moved around in the passenger seat.

The guy was barely pushing thirty. He looked lean and dapper. His black hair was cut high and tight. His face was chiseled and clean-shaven. He wore a crisp white button-up shirt with the sleeves rolled up, black pants, and matching dress shoes. He exuded confidence through his appearance and body language. Standing a foot shorter than him, the woman—his beloved wife—had curly black hair and gentle brown eyes. She was wearing a black maxi dress with a black blazer, which belonged to her husband, draped over her narrow shoulders. Her endearing smile revealed her kind, sincere personality.

Cindy didn't fall for her spell, though. In fact, as soon as she saw them, she *despised* the couple. She envied their relationship and wealth. She had only been observing them for a minute, but she already felt like she had known them for an eternity. The woman in the van was living her dream life while Cindy was stuck in her worst nightmare. The couple reminded her of Charlotte and her husband Michael. *Life really isn't fair,* she thought, bloody tears rimming her eyes like red eyeliner.

The woman exited the vehicle, then turned and opened the van's sliding door. The man went to her side. They fumbled about for a few seconds, then the guy gave her ass a gentle spanking. Suppressed laughter came out of the vehicle. The woman exited the van with a baby girl in her arms. The baby, swaddled in a warm blanket, was a little over a year old. She was whining and babbling, grouchy from the sudden awakening. Her head was rocking.

The woman smiled at her husband and said, "She's still sleepy. Go open the door before she really wakes up, Bryce. If she starts crying, *you're* going to spend the whole night getting her back to sleep."

"Yeah, yeah. I wouldn't want my girls to cry all night," Bryce replied. He patted her ass again, then made his way to the front door. While unlocking it, he furrowed his brow and patted his pockets. He glanced back at the van and said, "Sierra. Hey, *Sierra.*"

"What?" his wife responded, her voice just above a whisper.

"Grab my phone, will ya? I think it slipped out of my pocket."

"Not sure if you noticed, but my hands are kinda full over here," Sierra said as she approached him with their daughter in her arms and her purse slung over her shoulder. "I couldn't grab everything anyway. Get your phone and grab her diaper bag. I'll go put her to bed."

Bryce and Sierra, Cindy thought. *You're just the perfect couple, aren't you?*

She crept over to their house while staying hidden behind the picket fence. She watched as Bryce searched for his cell phone around the driver's seat. By the time he found it, Sierra was already inside the house. Bryce went to the other side of the van, grabbed the diaper bag, then shut the rolling door. While flicking his thumb across his cell phone's screen, he walked back to the porch.

Tracking his every step, Cindy whispered, "I can't miss my chance. No, no, no." Bryce opened the door and stepped inside. Cindy said, "No. I have to eat. *I have to eat.*"

She pushed the front gate open and, running on all fours, barreled up the walkway. Before Bryce could close the door behind him, she tackled it and forced herself into the home. The door swung open and crashed into a coat tree. Down the hall, Sierra gasped and hopped upon hearing the crashing noise. The baby started sobbing in her arms, once again annoyed by the interruption of her sleep.

Bryce flinched and yelled, "What the fuck?!"

He looked back at the doorway. He felt his heart drop into his stomach, setting off an explosion of nausea. Adrenaline told him to fight while anxiety forced him to freeze. He had never been in a situation like that before and he had never seen anyone like Cindy before. He walked backwards slowly, holding one arm out in front of him and the other behind him, using himself to block the intruder from reaching his family.

Cindy shambled into the home. She glanced around, wondering if there were any other people in the house. The archway to her right led to the living room. The parallel archway led to a dining room. Down the hall in front of her, she could see several doors and a staircase. She didn't see any alarm control panels in the foyer.

Bryce said, "Take whatever you want and leave. We won't try to stop you and–and we won't call the cops. Just don't do anything stupid, okay?"

Cindy snickered as she gazed into Bryce's eyes. She saw the unadulterated fear flowing through him. From over his shoulder, she could see Sierra was equally terrified, shuddering and stuttering as she struggled to comfort her baby. The infant continued bawling her eyes out.

"I want her," Cindy said as she closed the door behind her.

"He–Her?" Bryce stuttered.

"The baby. I want the baby."

Sierra said, "No. No, *never*. You can take our money, our credit cards, our furniture, but you are *not* taking my child."

"I've always wanted a baby."

"No! Bryce, do something!"

Bryce held his hands up, as if calling for peace, and said, "Calm down. Let's just all calm down." He looked Cindy over and said, "I don't think you want to do this. I can see that you're... You need help. You're, um... Look, I'm trying not to be offensive here, but I think you're on 'something.' And if you are, we can help you... I guess we can help you find help. Professional help. Seriously, you don't want to do this. You don't want our girl. Think about it. Please."

As if comforted by her father's soothing voice, the baby's sobs were reduced to some sleepy whimpers.

Cindy said, "I've thought about it my whole life. I've imagined living in a house like this, marrying a man like you, having a baby girl of my own... I have always wanted everything you have. I couldn't have it last year or the year before that or ever. I've always been so damn *fat* and *disgusting!*" She glared at Bryce and breathed loudly, then she giggled and looked down at herself. She said, "And look at me now! I'm worse than before!"

Bryce said, "Please calm down. Just relax, okay? We can talk about this. Let's... Let's just talk about this." He took two more steps back, then glanced over his shoulder and whispered, "Go into the nursery and lock yourself in. Call 911 and don't come–"

"Look at me!" Cindy interrupted. "Look at me, you bastard! I'm a monster! But it doesn't matter to you, does it? You don't really want to help me. It's bullshit. It's always bullshit. You're just waiting until the police show up so they can gun me down, aren't you? Well, you should see what I did to the last guy who thought the police were going to rescue him. I'm going to live no matter what. You? I'm not sure about you."

"Do whatever you want to me."

"Bryce, we have to run," Sierra said.

"But please leave my wife and daughter out of this," Bryce continued. "They're inno–"

Cindy sprinted down the hall. She leapt onto him, sending him plummeting to the floor. The floorboards rattled and squealed and groaned under their weight. Without a second thought, Cindy bit Bryce's neck. The night of violence had turned her into an efficient killer —*an apex predator*.

Bryce went down screaming and fighting. He bombarded the intruder with punches to the ribs and head. Yet, Cindy's grip on his neck remained firm. He grabbed her chin in one hand and clawed at her forehead with the other, trying to pry her mouth open. But her jaw was slammed shut with the strength of a crocodile. His eyes rolled up. He saw Sierra standing in the hallway.

Run, he wanted to yell, but only blood streamed out from the corners of his mouth.

Sierra watched the violent attack in awe. Her limbs locked up and her feet felt heavier. Their baby started crying again. She looked at her child, then at Bryce, and then back at the child. She screamed and ran down the hall. She stumbled up the stairs, then entered the first room to her left on the second floor.

Bryce felt a sense of relief upon hearing the door slam and a lock *click* upstairs. Cindy lifted her head and tore a piece of muscle off the left side of his neck. Blood geysered from his jugular and filled the cavity. Bryce coughed some up, too. He grabbed her throat and gave it a squeeze. Cindy spit his muscle out, then chomped down on his neck again.

A dew of cold sweat coated Bryce's forehead. He struggled to take in his short, shallow breaths. He clenched his eyes shut and ground his teeth as tightly as possible, face contorted in an expression of extreme anguish. He felt her teeth moving in his neck, grinding against his Adam's apple. The pain and traumatic loss of blood sent him into hemorrhagic shock.

Cindy tore his Adam's apple out. Her cheek ballooned out as she chewed on it, as if she were sucking on a massive jawbreaker. She inspected the big holes on Bryce's neck and thought: *He's a goner.* She left him there, twitching and croaking. She swallowed his mushy Adam's apple as she went up the stairs. Once again, the rush of murder revitalized her.

Death brought her closer to life.

At the top of the stairs, Cindy leaned next to the wall beside the first door to her left. She could hear Sierra and the baby crying in the room.

She smiled smugly and said, "I know you're in there, sweetie. You wouldn't jump out a window with your baby and you wouldn't leave without your man. I only saw you for a few minutes, but I already know the type of person you are." She moaned as she seductively sucked the blood off her fingers. She said, "You should come out here. Come take a look at your 'sweet' husband."

"Leave us alone!" Sierra shouted. "I called the cops! They're coming! They... They're coming..."

She coddled her baby and dropped to her knees near the door. Her cell phone was on the floor next to her. She had just confirmed her address with a 911 operator when Cindy's voice caused her to drop the phone. The call was still connected, but she couldn't hear the operator.

She was in the nursery—a room with baby blue walls and a dark blue carpet. A padded floor mat with a variety of zoo animals covered the center of the room. A sofa with a blanket hugged the wall to her left. To her right, there was a rocking chair and a crib. There were some shelves with children's books and chests with toys in the corners of the room. Parallel from the door, moonlight entered the room through a window overlooking the backyard.

Despite her daughter's incessant wailing, she had

heard most of Bryce's suffering. She didn't know what else to say to the intruder. She didn't want to believe her husband was dead.

Cindy knocked on the door and said, "Open up and I'll make this easier for you. Trust me, hon, I've busted doors down like this one before. And I can do it again. It wouldn't be very hard, especially with all of this fancy furniture you have around here."

Sierra didn't respond. Cindy could hear her panting and the baby's cries, though. She didn't have time to negotiate. She grabbed a sturdy console table in the hall, then using it as a battering ram, she thrust it at the door. The door creaked and shook. She stepped back, then she ran forward and rammed the table against the door again. The *bang* from the blow echoed through the house. With the third hit, the door flew open.

"Here's Cindy!" the intruder exclaimed. She laughed and said, "I love that line."

Weeping hysterically now, Sierra scrambled to the other side of the room. In a last-ditch effort to survive, she tried to open the window so she could jump out with her child. She couldn't open it with the baby in her arms, though, and she refused to let her go for even a second.

"*Stop,*" Cindy said sternly as she entered the nursery. "Seriously, you're just wasting my time and your energy. Don't make me do this the hard way. I've done that enough already. Besides, I feel... like I'm almost getting better. I don't need much more from you."

Sierra stopped her desperate attempt to escape. She turned around and checked every corner of the room, searching for another viable exit. But she was cornered.

Cindy looked at the crib, then she ran her eyes over the rest of the room. She said, "This room is... *beautiful*. You did a good job for her. A great job, really." She touched the wall over the crib and said, "This color reminds me of the sky. I bet that's why you chose it. Kids should aspire to fly. I would have picked the same color."

Sierra sniffled and stammered, "Wha–Wha–What do you want from me?"

"I want food."

"Please don't play these games with me. What do you want from me?"

"Food."

"Goddammit, there's food in the kitchen! Take whatever you want and leave!"

Cindy said, "I need different... food. I need blood. I need flesh. That's what makes me feel better. So, there are two things that can happen here right now. You can give yourself to me, then I'll leave. *Or* I'll kill you and your baby forcefully, then I'll leave. What's it going to be?"

Sierra was speechless. She looked down at her baby, saddened. The girl babbled and whined, spewing a stream of incomprehensible baby talk. The young mother stroked her child's short black hair. A tear fell from her eye and plopped on the girl's cheek. Although she wasn't fully aware of her surroundings, the baby felt her mother's anxiety. She whined and wiggled in her mother's arms, uncomfortable and scared.

Sierra nodded reluctantly. Her options were limited. She thought about fighting back, but if Bryce couldn't overpower the intruder, she figured she didn't stand a chance against Cindy. It had been about five minutes since she reported the home invasion. Although she didn't hear any sirens in the neighborhood, she hoped the cops would show up in the nick of time to save her daughter. Like most good mothers, she was willing to sacrifice herself for her child.

She kissed the baby's forehead, then she carefully placed her in the crib. The infant squirmed around on her back, searching for comfort.

"I love you," Sierra whispered into the girl's ear. She looked at Cindy and, with her voice breaking, she said, "Her name is Alaina. She's... fourteen months old. She's a good girl. A sweet, precious, beautiful... innocent girl. Please don't hurt her. Do whatever you want to me, but don't hurt my daughter."

"Don't worry about her," Cindy said. "I would *never* hurt a baby. Besides, I'll be out of here as soon as I'm done with you. I don't plan on waiting for the police. And hey, chances are your neighbors are going to drop by and find Alaina here as soon as I leave. If they're anything like my neighbors, they love drama but don't want to get involved until *after* the fact."

"Fa–Fine... Fine..."

Sierra dropped to her knees next to the cradle. She could see Alaina from the corner of her eye. She started having second thoughts, but it was too late. She shrieked as the intruder sank her teeth into her neck. Her ear-splitting scream blew through the house and reached the front lawn and backyard. In less than ten seconds, her screaming stopped and she began to gargle her own blood. And in less than thirty seconds, the ruckus from the struggle ended abruptly.

Tranquility returned to the neighborhood.

Like her husband, Sierra was left with her throat torn open. Tubes and veins and muscles were visible in the gaping wound on her neck. Cindy's face was painted red with the blood. Some drops landed on her balding scalp, too. She towered over the crib and cast her eyes at the baby. Alaina's cries sounded different now. She didn't cry out of annoyance or discomfort. She sobbed out of bereavement. She didn't fully understand the concept of death, but she *felt* her mother's demise.

"It's okay," Cindy said softly. "Everything's okay now."

She carried Alaina out of the room. Downstairs, she casually stepped over Bryce's dead body and made her way to the front porch. The porch light dawned on her, illuminating her scars and wounds and deformities with a white glow. Despite her appearance, she felt stronger than ever—more *confident* than ever. She stared at the baby and thought: *How far can I go to survive?*

"I can't stop now," she whispered.

She heard emergency sirens in the distance, gradually growing louder. She hurried past the front gate, then took a left on the sidewalk. She only passed the neighboring house before the baby began to bawl, as if competing with the sirens. Cindy rocked her from side to side while shushing her. Alaina kept crying, though.

"This isn't going to work if you don't stop crying, honey," Cindy whispered.

She glanced over her shoulder upon hearing the clear *whoop* of a police siren. The police had reached the neighborhood. She held Alaina closer to her chest to smother her cries. She ran past two more houses, crossed the street, then took another left. She jogged next to a brick partition separating the houses from the sidewalk.

Halfway down the block, she crouched behind a truck parked on the street and checked on Alaina. The baby was fidgeting and fussing. Her brown eyes resembled her mother's.

Cindy frowned and said, "You're so beautiful. I wish it didn't have to be this way. You would have been the perfect daughter. But I have to get out of here and I need more... more 'power,' I guess. I *have* to do this.

You haven't lived very long anyway. You can't..." She coughed to clear her throat, then said, "You can't fight for a future you never even thought about. You can't cherish a life you've never actually lived."

Alaina continued crying while twisting and turning in the woman's arms. She had a look of fear in her wide, teary eyes and her lips were pale, as if she had just seen a ghost—as if she had just realized the truth. She was conscious of her parents' deaths, and she felt the malevolence within her kidnapper. Despite her age, she knew something had gone terribly wrong.

Cindy said, "I'm sorry, baby. I'm so sorry."

She pushed Alaina's face closer to her sagging bosom. The baby's cries were stifled. Cindy drew a deep, raspy breath, then she chomped into the top of Alaina's head. Blood gushed out of the soft spot on her head—the anterior fontanelle—like lava from an erupting volcano. It hit the back of Cindy's throat with enough pressure to make her gag.

Rattling and hiccuping noises came out of Alaina's mouth. Blood spurted out of the hole on her head and raced across her face. She was barely clinging to life.

Upon regaining her breath, Cindy bit into Alaina's head again. Her teeth broke her soft bones and penetrated her brain.

The baby went silent.

Cindy gnawed on Alaina's head, reducing it to mush, then she sucked up the pieces—her hair, her skin, her broken bones, her brain. She swallowed it, then she forced more of the baby's skull into her mouth. After choking down more bone, brain, and hair, she amputated Alaina's left eye with the third bite. She chomped away at her head, munching and slurping.

In less than two minutes, she devoured the top half of Alaina's head. Her skull was turned into a bowl with a jagged rim, filled with pulpy brain and blood. The top halves of her ears were gone and only the bottom half of her nose remained attached to her face.

Cindy was about to take another bite when she heard a siren on the street behind her. She looked over her shoulder and saw a patrol car race past an intersection. She was out of time. She glanced at the partition to her right, then at the truck to her left.

She said, "I'm sorry, but it's–"

She started coughing. She held her clenched fist over her mouth to try to suppress the noise, but each cough was more painful and harsher than the last. Then she felt a lump climb up her throat. She choked on it for a few seconds, then hacked up a thick hairball. It landed on the sidewalk. Drenched in blood and saliva, most of it was Alaina's hair, but there was some cat fur in the mix.

Cindy slapped her chest while gasping for air. After recomposing herself, she put the baby's corpse under the truck.

She whispered, "I'm sorry, but it's going to be okay. You'll see your parents in heaven."

She waited there for a moment, as if expecting the dead baby to respond. She heard another purring engine and saw red and blue lights in the periphery of her vision. Another patrol car sped past the intersection. She ran into a nearby alley and vanished in the darkness.

18

FAIRY TALE ENDING

CINDY SMILED AS SHE STARED DOWN AT HERSELF. SHE wore a white button-up shirt tucked into a tight black skirt, black stockings, and matching high heels. Her stomach was flat and firm, her breasts were perky, and her hips were wide. She saw herself as 'plus-sized' and 'thick'—labels she preferred over 'fat.' Her lush, wavy blonde hair reached her shoulders.

Time healed all wounds.

She glanced around the room. The seminar hall had beige walls and dark blue carpeting from wall to wall. In front of her, there were two columns of desks with green tablecloths. Each table sat three people. Behind her, there were two white boards and a projection screen. There was a podium with a microphone next to her.

She glanced over at the tall windows to her left,

peering past the crimson curtains. She saw people walking on the beach and splashing in the water. The bright sun sparkled on the waves rolling towards the shore. People sat under large umbrellas at lunch tables, sipping on margaritas while gossiping. The atmosphere was serene.

A *clap* echoed through the seminar hall, disrupting the silence.

Cindy looked at the double doors at the other end of the room. A man in a black suit had entered the seminar hall. His hair was slicked back and cut short on the sides. He had a strong jaw of well-groomed stubble. There was a small mole on his left cheek. The wide PR grin on his face screamed: *I'm a salesman!*

"May I help you?" Cindy asked in a calm, confident tone.

Walking down the center aisle, the man said, "Hello, Ms. Moore. My name is Robert Ryan. It's a pleasure to finally meet you. I've been trying to contact you for some time now. You know, it's very difficult to keep track of you. One day, you're in a beautiful resort in the US. The next, you're holding a conference in Hong Kong. Then the day after that, you're back in a resort in Mexico. But I've finally caught up to you. *Finally*."

"Well, Mr. Ryan, as you clearly know, I'm a busy person. So, how may I help you?"

"Straight to business. I like that. I listened to your seminar and, I must say, it was wonderful."

"Is that so? My audience usually consists of young

women, so it's rare that I see a man like yourself around here. I don't think I've ever been approached by a man after any of my seminars, actually."

Robert reached the podium. He said, "That's interesting. You said 'audience' just now, didn't you?"

"Yes, I did. What's so interesting about that?"

"That's not accurate, is it? You meant 'clients,' right? Or perhaps a better term for them would be... 'suckers.' Wouldn't you agree?"

Robert gave her a cocky smile, then turned his attention to the whiteboards. Notes and numbers were scribbled on the boards in black marker. The figures represented statistics concerning a miracle weight loss supplement. A question was scrawled across the top of one of the whiteboards. It read: *How much can you lose with one capsule?*

Cindy squinted an eye at the guy. She couldn't tell if he was trying to be funny or if he was just arrogant. His prying tone made him sound like a member of law enforcement.

She asked, "Suckers? What exactly are you suggesting by that, Mr. Ryan?"

Robert stared at Cindy with a deadpan expression, then he cracked another smile and said, "You know exactly what I mean. To them, to your 'audience,' it's not so clear. But to everyone else—to people who know the business, people who *work* in the business—it's as clear as the sun on a summer day. A summer day like today, for example." He leaned in closer to her and whispered, "It's a pyramid scheme."

Cindy narrowed her other eye and leaned away from her visitor. She operated a questionable business, but she stood by her product.

She said, "I don't know what you're talking about. I run a legitimate business with plenty of opportunities for advancement. If you're here to question me about something, I think you should talk to my lawyer first."

Robert responded, "Oh, don't get me wrong. I'm not that guy from the FTC looking to bust you. No, I actually want to congratulate you. I'm also here to talk business. I'd like to offer you a lucrative opportunity on behalf of my company, *Weight and See*. I'm sure men in suits have wasted your time before, but I think we can offer you something bigger. First, I just need a few details about your business. I already know quite a bit to be honest, but I need to clarify a few things. Can we have a chat?"

Cindy gazed into Robert's shiny blue eyes. She was more curious than cautious. She nodded in agreement.

———

Waves clashed at the shore with a soothing rhythm. Children screamed and giggled with joy as they scampered across the beach. Families set up beach blankets, umbrellas, chairs, and coolers while couples took romantic strolls with the rippling water splashing at their feet.

Cindy and Robert sat at a table outside, hiding from the sun in the shade of a large umbrella. Robert had removed his jacket and rolled up the sleeves of his button-up shirt. He sipped a margarita while the breeze cooled his sweaty skin.

He loosened his tie, then said, "It's like I've been saying, Cindy—may I call you Cindy?"

"Sure."

"It's like I've been saying, Cindy, I know quite a bit about your business. We've been watching you. Don't let that alarm you, though. It's perfectly normal to keep your eyes on the competition. I'm sure you've heard of us and you've seen the way we move."

"I have."

"Now we want to offer you something special, but we want to make sure we know what we're getting into. You sell diet pills, right? Well, your 'employees' sell diet pills, *right?*"

Cindy looked out at the sea and said, "Diet *capsules* to be exact."

"How? We've ran our own calculations and, even with our most conservative estimates, your sales numbers are astounding. And you're seeing steady, nonstop growth. Your sales network is... Well, it's amazing. What's so special about your company? Hmm? That is, if you're not all talk."

"What's so special about it? Well, for one, we don't

sell dreams, we sell solutions. We sell *real* miracles. Our supplement actually works, unlike most of the other crap on the market, and the proof is in the pudding. That's why it sells so well."

"That makes sense. So, what exactly is in these miracle capsules?"

Cindy laughed, then said, "You're a charming man, Robert, but that doesn't mean I'm going to give you the world on a silver platter. If your offer is as lucrative as you say it is, I'll reveal some of my secrets *after* the ink dries on some paperwork. I sure as hell wouldn't tell you just so you can leave this resort with my golden egg. That's *not* happening."

Robert was taken aback by her hostile tone. He saw the ferocity in her eyes. She didn't look like a violent person on the surface, but she seemed prepared to get her hands dirty.

"I get ya," Robert said. "I suppose we'll have to sign a few NDAs before we get that far. Can you tell me about your network, though? If we were to buy you out, we'd have to know who we'd be adopting."

Shifting to a friendlier tone, Cindy said, "It's simple, really. It's pretty much the same model many businesses use nowadays. I find aspiring models on Instagram and Facebook. You know, the type with curvy bodies, skimpy clothes, and revealing photos in their feeds. The type that show *everything* to get a few followers. The type that claim they're making millions of dollars and traveling the world as entrepreneurs but can't really prove any of it. I'm sure you've seen them around before. I pick the ones with the largest social media followings and those with a clear desire for money. You know they love money when they pose with stacks of cash that doesn't belong to them in their pictures or they frequently fly to Dubai on 'business' trips. I offer them an opportunity to lose a little bit of weight and a chance to be rich—*real* rich."

"That's it?"

"Of course. Occasionally, it takes some convincing, but, like I said, the supplement itself does most of the work. These models lose weight, they share their progress, then they sell the capsules to their followers. The capsules work for their customers, too. They end up sharing pictures of their results and the cycle continues. There is no better marketing than word of mouth. A lot of customers end up being desperate men looking for some sort of acknowledgement from our 'models,' but that doesn't really matter, does it? The capsules work for them, too, and money is money."

Her formula for success was tried and tested. Demographics were a significant variable, but the truth was universal: Sexual imagery sold products. Whether it was men buying products advertised by sexy women or women buying products to *become* sexy women, sex was a significant ingredient in marketing for many industries. Dietary supplements were dreams sold by people with dream physiques.

"Money is money," Robert repeated as he nodded.

He leaned back in his chair and glanced around the beach. He said, "I think I've heard enough, Cindy. At least, I've heard enough in this place. I'd like to continue this conversation in a more proper environment. Somewhere with air conditioning."

"I'd like to hear your offer now if that's okay," Cindy answered. "I'm a very busy woman. I don't have time to waste."

"There are some details we still have to iron out, but I'd say the offer is as simple as your business model. Your company becomes part of the Weight and See family. We'd offer you mass production of your product and expand your reach to regions around the world. You wouldn't have to worry about expenses anymore. That would be our responsibility. And although I love what you're doing with the word-of-mouth marketing, you'd have access to our advertising teams. We can get *real* models and celebrities to partner with us. You'll obviously get a hefty payout upfront, but we're also interested in keeping you on board. Imagine the money we'd make if we combined our strengths with your business acumen."

Cindy smiled and said, "You sure know how to woo a woman. I'm interested, but I have some conditions."

"Like I said, we can iron out the smaller details in a more formal environment."

"No. Before we even start negotiating, I want your word on something."

"I'm not sure I can give it to you, but... shoot."

"I must remain at the forefront of the business and at the top of my pyramid."

Robert raised his brow at her. He expected her to demand money—lots and lots of money—as well as power. Her request was unusually simple.

He said, "I suppose that shouldn't be a problem, especially if the numbers you're boasting are real." He wagged his finger at her and said, "But now you've got me all curious. If you don't mind me asking, why would you want to be the face of the business? Usually, the real money makers hide out in the background. We work the show like puppet-masters. It seems to me like you want to be the puppet *and* the puppet-master. Why?"

"I'm no puppet. It's more like... I want to be the *director* and the *lead actress*. I went through quite a bit to get to my position, and I don't want my journey to be in vain. You see, before I started this business, these capsules were too strong. I looked like, well, *shit*. I got skinnier, but those results came with a hefty price. I lost everything. I almost lost myself. That was over four years ago, though. I tweaked the recipe. It's less effective now, but it's a whole lot safer."

She thought about her first experience with the miracle capsules and her journey to operating a successful business of her own. With Deki dead, she adopted his business thanks to his contacts, which she found in his cell phone. Blackmail and the threat of violence brought her far in life. And with compensation from Deki's business partners, she was able to afford extensive reconstructive surgery while hiding from the authorities. And, due to Cindy's transformation, the police investigation was complicated by unreliable DNA evidence.

She spent a lot of time thinking about her past actions. She was racked with guilt during her recovery, praying to God—to any God—for forgiveness. But after taking a turn for the better, she reverted to her selfish self. The only noticeable difference to her was that she sounded more like the little voice that she used to hear in her head. The violence and tragedy didn't haunt her. She could look a baby in the eye without a shred of regret or guilt. Instead, her past helped her hone her predatory business sense.

Interrupting her contemplation, Robert said, "I see. I didn't realize you used your own program. As long as it's safe, I think we can make everything work. You'll be the lead actress, you'll be the director, and we'll all share in the fruits of success. Sound good?"

Cindy said, "Perfect."

"Well, we should schedule a meeting. I'd like you to come to my office so we can get this paperwork done. I'm excited to call you our partner, Cindy. Let's expand our network. Let's sell these capsules worldwide. You ready to get rich?"

Cindy shook his hand in a gesture of agreement. Despite her own experience, she had no qualms about spreading the potentially fatal capsules around the globe.

With a mischievous smile and a devious twinkle in her eyes, she said, "I've been waiting for this moment my whole life. Let's rock this world."

JOIN THE MAILING LIST

Need to lose some weight? Looking for that special 'miracle' weight loss capsule? Well, you won't get it from me. I can, however, provide you with dozens of horror books. Want to read some more body horror like this one? Looking for a gory slasher? Maybe a horrific coming-of-age tale? How about a violent revenge story? Or maybe a couple of books about the infamous snuff industry? I've published over 50 horror books and I continue to publish new stories frequently. I believe I have something for everyone. I think you'll especially enjoy my stories if you like going into dark, taboo territory.

If you enjoyed this novel or my writing style and you'd like to learn more about my books and stay up to date with my latest releases, I strongly recommend you sign up for my mailing list. By signing up, you'll ensure that you won't miss out on my newest books or my *huge* book sales—which I host often. I usually send one email a month, but you may receive two or three during busier months—or none at all if I have nothing going on in my writing career. And that's what this is all about: *Books.* You won't receive any spam with blog posts, life updates (unless there's a serious emergency), or my political views. And it's completely *free.* Visit this link to sign up: http://eepurl.com/bNl1CP.

DEAR READER

Hello to you first-time readers and hello *again* to you die-hard returning fans. I started this huge, daunting Author's Enhanced Edition process in early 2021 with the rewrite of *Camp Blaze*. It still feels a little strange to be revisiting my old books, rewriting nearly everything from the ground up—including these letters. But here we are. You asked for more enhanced editions, and I'm happy to give them to you. (And for the first time in paperback! Hello, paperback readers! Imagine a waving emoji right here.)

Bad Appetites was inspired by the body horror genre. Originally, its main inspirations were John Carpenter's *The Thing* and David Cronenberg's *The Fly*. There's something about watching ungodly transformations that just fascinates and frightens me. For the author's enhanced edition, I was also inspired to come back to this story after watching Brandon Cronenberg's

Possessor. Meanwhile, when I commissioned the cover illustration for this book, I was inspired by the visuals from 1977's *The Incredible Melting Man.*

I was also inspired by drugs. I think dietary supplements are scary. I've never heard of a diet pill causing a person to liquefy, but I've read about these things causing heart and liver problems as well as other serious issues. At the same time, I had been reading about a street drug called 'krokodil'—a flesh-eating drug that can cause gangrene. So, I started thinking: *What if someone made a homemade dietary supplement that had terrible side effects like krokodil?* And that was how this book came about.

The author's enhanced edition brought this story's word count from approximately 46,000 to over 59,000. You're probably wondering how the word count increased or if I just padded it out for the sake of making it longer. In 2016—back when this book was originally written—I was a different writer in a different setting. Back then, certain books were being removed from store shelves due to the nature of their content or even their titles. (I suppose that's still happening today, but I digress.) So, being a new(ish) writer with a small fanbase at the time, I made cuts in order to avoid getting banned.

What you read now is not only a technically improved version of the original story but a *complete* version. I rewrote some of the scenes that were toned down and reimplemented scenes that were cut out.

That's why the book is longer. I also took the opportunity to flesh out the characters and dialogue. Despite the far-fetched concept, I wanted to give the characters more layers to give it a more realistic feel. This was my original vision for the book, and I'm glad I could finally share it with you.

If you enjoyed this book, please make your voice heard and leave an honest review on Amazon, Goodreads, Bookbub, and your blogs and vlogs. Take a minute to share it on Facebook, Twitter, Instagram, and TikTok. Your reviews help me improve and give me the spark I need to keep writing. By sharing my book on social media, you also help me reach more readers. Like I've always said, reviews and word-of-mouth are crucial parts to an independent author's success. I probably wouldn't be here if it weren't for you.

If you need help writing your review, try answering questions like these: Did you enjoy the book? Was it shocking and/or entertaining? Would you like to read another body horror story from me? Would you take Deki's miracle weight loss capsule? Good or bad, short or detailed, your reviews are very helpful. I unfortunately don't have the time to respond to each review, but I want to thank you for sharing your thoughts and continuing to support me.

I'm writing this letter on December 6th, 2021. There's not much going on in my personal life. I'm still on a social media hiatus, only dropping by every now and then. I still love reading your comments and talking to all of you, though. Seriously, you're the best part of social media for me. I've been feeling a little homesick recently. I'm still in Japan, so it's been about 21 months since I've been in the US or seen my family. I was hoping to visit in early 2022, but it looks like the situation is still volatile. On the bright side, at least it doesn't feel like the end of the world anymore, so I'm not pouting or whining too much.

I'm focused on my writing, which is going well. After this, I'll be jumping right into *When She Weeps*, which is slated to release in May 2022. It's a non-supernatural reimagining of the Weeping Woman/La Llorona urban legend. I've been studying cartels and watching some of their videos to prepare for this book. At the moment, it's looking like it might come in at over 100,000 words, making it my longest book to date. But it's still early, so things might get cut. Keep that in mind. Once I'm finished with that, I'll finish up the next author's enhanced edition: *The Harbinger of Vengeance*. I'll share more details on that one later, but I can say now that it has received the biggest upgrade yet. Then it's time to share a very disturbing, provocative project that I've been working on since 2018... *The President's Son*. A lot of experimental stuff is coming, so I'm excited and anxious about the future. Hope you'll be sticking with me!

Finally, if you enjoyed this book, go check out my Amazon's Author page. I've published over 50 novels.

Like I mentioned in my pitch for my newsletter, I've dabbled in nearly every subgenre—body horror, slasher, psychological, dystopian, supernatural, revenge, coming-of-age. And I continue to break new ground every year. If you're looking for a grim, balls-to-the-wall slasher, check out *Do Not Disturb* and its recently released sequel *Do Not Disturb 2: The Platinum Palace.* And like I mentioned earlier, *When She Weeps* is due in May 2022. If you love my twisted romance stories, you're not going to want to miss this one. As usual, I appreciate all of the love and support. Thank you for reading!

Until our next venture into the dark and disturbing,

Jon Athan

P.S. If you have any questions or comments, feel free to contact me directly using my business email: info@jon-athan.com. You can also contact me through Twitter @Jonny_Athan, my Facebook page, or Instagram @AuthorJonnyAthan. I can't promise you that I'll reply right away, but I always *try* to respond. Thanks!

Made in United States
Cleveland, OH
22 December 2024

12553479R00166